W9-CPX-220

The Forbidden Purple City

 PHILIP HUYNH

The
Forbidden
Purple City

stories

Copyright © 2019 by Philip Huynh.

All rights reserved. No part of this work may be reproduced or used in any form
or by any means, electronic or mechanical, including photocopying, recording,
or any retrieval system, without the prior written permission of the publisher or
a licence from the Canadian Copyright Licensing Agency (Access Copyright).
To contact Access Copyright, visit www.accesscopyright.ca or call 1-800-893-5777.

Edited by Bethany Gibson.
Cover and page design by Julie Scriver.
Cover adapted from "Hanoi Traffic Milieu" by Ian on unsplash.com.
Printed in Canada.
10 9 8 7 6 5 4 3 2 1

Library and Archives Canada Cataloguing in Publication

Huynh, Philip, 1975-, author
The Forbidden Purple City / Philip Huynh.

Short stories.
Issued in print and electronic formats.
ISBN 978-1-77310-078-4 (softcover).--ISBN 978-1-77310-079-1 (EPUB).--
ISBN 978-1-77310-080-7 (Kindle)

I. Title.

PS8615.U96F67 2019   C813'.6   C2018-904607-4
                                             C2018-904608-2

Goose Lane Editions acknowledges the generous financial support
of the Government of Canada, the Canada Council for the Arts,
and the Province of New Brunswick.

Goose Lane Editions
500 Beaverbrook Court, Suite 330
Fredericton, New Brunswick
CANADA E3B 5X4
www.gooselane.com

RECYCLED
Paper made from
recycled material
FSC® C103567

To my parents, and to Sowon, Margo, and Oona.

Thus, it's not you
but I who must ask why the sea eats so many fires
or how a drop of salt water contains each moment.

— Philip Levine, "Blue and Blue"

Contents

The Investment
on Dumfries Street

I never saw my father again after leaving Vancouver five years ago, in our beat-up Corolla bound for Los Angeles. I kept meaning to come back to visit, but I just never got around to it, and the days passed. I slept in my Corolla on Santa Monica Beach while bussing tables until I could afford to rent a tiny pad, meanwhile auditioning for bit parts. I sold the Corolla when I lost my bussing job, all the while auditioning for more bit parts. I was scared of crossing the border to see my father in case I wouldn't be able to cross back to America.

In many ways my father was a typical Vietnamese man of his generation. Part of the war-ravaged, drop-everything-you're-doing, forget-about-that-rubber-plantation-you-own, hop-on-this-boat-and-hightail-it-across-the-Pacific generation—a generation that was weary of the naïveté of my own. He wanted me to become a businessman when I grew up and was disappointed when I chose something as imprudent as acting. "Why spend a life pretending to be other people?" he asked. "Why not just be yourself?"

Had we not lost the war to the North Vietnamese, my father would have inherited his father's rubber plantation, which, my father tells me, had enough rubber sap for all the tires on Highway 1. Instead, my father worked as a short-order cook at a diner on Southeast Marine Drive, a wooden shack with a corrugated tin roof. But cooking was just a gig, his "front" until he could find the right business partner and close on the right deal. Evidence of these business partners and deals for the most part eluded me.

We were stuck in a one-bedroom apartment off Fraser and Kingsway, and my father never stopped reaching upwards, grasping for something that he believed already belonged to him. He was a tenacious practitioner of positive thinking, and believed that every misfortune was necessary, part of the winding road towards his eventual restoration. Even living in shabby East Vancouver was a good thing as he saw it, though the well-to-do lived along western waterfronts or on mountainsides. "We just got off the boat," said my father. "Why stop at the beach? Keep moving."

My father schemed to the grave. After I left home, he would pitch his business ideas to me over the phone, full of faith that one would finally, at the age of sixty, sixty-two, sixty-five, make him a killing. He spoke of acquiring a stake in a raspberry farm in Surrey, opening his own Swiss Chalet outlet, participating in various complicated real-estate Ponzi schemes. He developed all these ideas while on his cigarette breaks. His pitches always started with "I met a diner today. We've become good friends..." His enthusiasm never wavered, but even over the phone I could tell that his health was deteriorating as the months went by. I only half-listened to his ideas, knowing that what he was pitching one day would be replaced by something else the next. My attention would wander until snapped back by the gunshot coughing that punctuated my father's ruminations. "I'm fine, I'm fine," he would say. "I get excited sometimes."

I know of only one deal that he acted on. When I was fifteen, my father told me about a house he'd bought on Dumfries Street in a tree-filled neighbourhood south of where we lived. He picked me up after school one day in our Corolla and drove me by the house. It was a Vancouver Special, one of those local confections, two storeys of vanilla stucco and brick, topped by terra-cotta. A unibrow balcony stretched from one end of the house to the other. The front yard rolled gently uphill.

"That's big for just us," I said. "How'd you get the money?"

"We're not living there," he said. "It's an investment. I got it with something called leverage. You'll learn about that when you are in business school. I have a partner. We'll sell it when it's worth something more. That's called profit."

I met my father's business partner, a slender man named Sonny Ngo who sported too-tight acid-washed jeans. My father was a short, slight man, but Sonny was even shorter and slighter. He wore a silver thumbtack in his left ear, had a chip in his front tooth, and drove a black Camaro. He wore cruddy black sneakers with white socks that his jeans didn't cover. I saw him a few times in my father's diner and Sonny always ordered a Coke for me. "On me," he said, even though I was always fed for free there. When he flashed his chipped tooth at me, I took the gesture as an obscenity.

There was a change in my father for the two years that he was invested in that house. During this time he would occasionally go on a spending binge. He loved suits even though he never had a reason to wear them. He bought suits for me even though I had no reason to wear them. A few times he came home in a new suit that he'd bought at Tip Top Tailors, forced me to put a suit on too, and took me to the Keg on Granville Island. He ordered us two prime rib dinners on these occasions, closed his eyes in a silent prayer for my departed mother, and tried, without ever succeeding, to finish his meal. He gave me advice that made sense only on the most subliminal level: "You've got to be able to smell the cash before you can hold it in your hands," for example. He also bought me various businessman knick-knacks, such as a Waterman pen, an embossed leather day planner, a slim metallic briefcase.

Despite these binges, there was never any real change to the economy of our lives. We still lived in the small apartment where I slept on the Murphy bed in the living room, the kitchen faucet still leaked, and I packed my own sliced turkey or egg sandwiches for lunch every day. We ran out of closet space for the suits, fedoras, and Italian-leather shoes my father bought for himself; they were piled on top of a large cardboard box that blocked the sliding closet door. On the sly, I started selling some of these classy but useless things. I got rid of the Waterman pen and bought myself some fresh underwear. I sold a couple of my suits to pay off a plumber, to buy hand soap and enough toilet paper to avoid those challenging gap days, and to help pay the rent.

I entered the house on Dumfries Street only once, when I was seventeen, on the closing night of my school's production of *Burn This*. I played Pale, a cokehead restaurant manager whose gay brother had recently drowned. Pale was out of my character range. Since I was eleven I had gravitated towards quiet and smouldering roles, not crazy, wired characters. When the play was done, I felt tightly strung, like a fiddle with strings on the verge of snapping. I needed some fresh air and couldn't face the celebration dinner with the other actors. I bolted without even wiping all the white makeup from my face. I paced the residential streets of East Vancouver on my own.

I turned a corner onto Dumfries Street and came upon the house inadvertently; I had forgotten about it. The head of a lamppost was bent at a weird angle, casting a spotlight on a large rhododendron bush in the front yard, electrifying the already ebullient flowers into something gaudy, like a Christmas display in the spring. This was my father's investment.

I wondered what it would be like to live in a house so

large. Then I saw Sonny. He was on the balcony, sitting on a chair with his legs propped against the railing, smoking a cigarette. He waved at me like a prince.

"I left the front door unlocked," he called. "Let yourself up." I went inside and upstairs, and met him on the balcony. He flashed his chipped tooth and offered me a cigarette. I declined.

"You're worried I'll tell your dad?" he asked.

"I just don't smoke."

Sonny laughed. I asked him who the tenants were and he told me there weren't any. I had assumed this was where my father's extra income came from. I asked Sonny if he lived here and he shook his head.

"It's my work space," he said, and laughed again, a giggle really. "You want to see?"

He led me back inside and downstairs. We went through the living room, which was empty except for a couple of chairs, a mah-jong table, and a Q*bert, the classic tabletop arcade game that I painfully wanted to snatch. The dining room was empty except for a crystal chandelier and a clock radio on the floor. He led me down to the basement, where he said he kept his "prestige."

Behind a plastic curtain were row after row of brightly lit marijuana plants in black plastic pots. Overhead were the grow lights, nurturing the cannabis. The smell of the plants was meaty.

Sonny grabbed an old-fashioned perfume atomizer from the floor and tended to the weed with little sprays of mist. On bended knee he examined the spiky plants with thumb and forefinger, as if checking for a pulse. The finely articulated fan leaves formed a paw that seemed to hold on to Sonny's own.

"You got a joint?" I asked. "I could really use one right now." I wasn't serious, but Sonny didn't laugh.

"No way. No way," he said. "No lighting up on the grounds. Are you for real?"

I needed to get away from the stench of the marijuana. I told Sonny that I'd take him up on his offer of a cigarette. He took me to the backyard where there was a small grove of plum and cherry trees. He watched me like a warden while I dragged on the cigarette. After I finished, I shook his hand and made my way out through the back alley.

When I got home, I slammed the door hard but failed to wake up my father. I couldn't forgive him for associating with someone so truly ghetto as Sonny. Sure, my father and I were also poor, but we were different. Sonny, although born in Canada, was ghetto from day one. My father and I were rendered poor by unfortunate geopolitical circumstances. As deluded as my father's aspirations were, at least, I had once thought, he had always set his sights high. But in fact he was risking our liberty to be something as pedestrian as a marijuana farmer.

I had half a mind to call the cops. I may have even picked up the phone. I didn't make the call, and in the end I didn't need to. A few months later I walked by the house on Dumfries Street. The police had raided and taped it. My father was never approached because, as it turned out, his name had never been on the title. And Sonny never ratted him out.

When I turned eighteen, I sold the rest of my suits and even some of my father's. I left most of the cash for him, kept some for gas, and headed down to Los Angeles in the Corolla.

I mentioned the house on Dumfries Street just one time over the phone, and my father hung up on me. I never mentioned it again. I was curious, however, about the fate of Sonny. Just this year, in our last conversation, I asked my father about him.

"Sonny was an unsuitable partner," said my father. "He had ambition but was missing the other important thing. What's that word? It rhymes with ambition."

"Rhymes with ambition?" I asked. I couldn't think of it. There was a moment of silence as my father fumbled for the word.

"Discretion," said my father. "Sonny missed discretion. It's vital in a partner." I was too weary at this point to argue with my father over whether the words actually rhymed.

"What about contrition?" I asked. "Have you thought of that? Does that sound like it?"

My father became quiet long enough for me to worry about how much time I had left on my calling card. Finally, deliberately, he said, "What would that mean?"

I could not begin to explain with the time we had left.

Gulliver's Wife

When her husband Thuong told Josephine that Vancouver was bilingual, that it was just as French as it was English — like the rest of Canada — she believed him. There was no need to go to Montreal, where some of her friends had ended up. Vancouver would be as fine a place as any to continue life.

Until her last day in Saigon, Josephine taught French in a primary school, refusing to admit that French would be useless to her students once the Communists took over. Her great regret was never getting to see any of them discover *L'Étranger*. But at least she got to leave Vietnam in an airplane, not like her friends. She fled to Hong Kong with Thuong and his mother. Thuong would return to studying economics now that his military career was finished. In the year they spent in Hong Kong, while Thuong applied to universities all over the free world, Josephine picked up more Cantonese than English, though all she could really do in Cantonese was haggle down the price of vegetables.

Two universities in the Vancouver area offered Thuong scholarships. All else being equal, Thuong chose the school located in the mountains because such a school is, naturally, more auspicious than a school by the sea. When they arrived, Josephine noticed that the only thing French about Vancouver was the bilingual grocery labels.

Now, seven years on, their son, Christian, set for kindergarten, the family rents a basement suite on Fleming Street in East Vancouver, and Thuong is still working on his PhD. Josephine's English is much improved, although she still prefers to read the grocery labels in French. She occasionally watches the French broadcast of the CBC, even though the Québécois accent will always sound foreign. Maybe it is just as well that they ended up in Vancouver instead of Montreal.

...

Josephine sits in with Christian for the first few days of school, because he is a weeper when she leaves him alone. She doesn't like what she sees. She understands that in public school the children don't wear uniforms, but most boys here don't even wear collars. In Vietnam even the poor wore uniforms with stiff collars, even if they only owned one shirt that their mothers had to iron each morning. And everything here is in English. Nothing is taught in French. Josephine pulls Christian out of kindergarten after only two weeks.

There is a Catholic school close to home. She had not considered St. Maurice's earlier because it charged tuition—a few hundred dollars and the cost of a uniform.

They will have to budget better if Christian is to go. For dinner there will be fewer noodles in each bowl of pho. She will have to cut the beef into thinner slices. But it will be worth it. St. Maurice's teaches French.

The French language conjures up everything Josephine is fond of about Vietnam, of grey-green margouillats climbing the Doric columns of the school where she taught, of nuns chewing betel quid while tracing their sisters' steps across the courtyard, of ham and baguettes. What happens to wine when it is allowed to breathe in the open air? Josephine is not an expert on wines, but she imagines it is similar to the alchemy that occurs in her head when she inhales French. French takes her back home more than Vietnamese does. Vietnamese, these days, is the language of arguments over chores and the future.

...

No one notices them when they enter the classroom at St. Maurice's. The class is held in a portable soaked in the musty smell of plaster, wet wool, and rain-drenched wood. The French kindergarten teacher is writing on the chalkboard: *le chat, le chien, au pays,* and other short words arranged like little bonbons on a plate. The teacher's back is to the pupils, who are scattered throughout the classroom among the books, toys, and cubbyholes.

Josephine sits on a Popsicle-orange chair in the corner and Christian stands by her side, his hand on her shoulder. The teacher turns around and calls the children to attention, ignorant of Josephine's presence.

There are many things here that remind Josephine of her classroom in Vietnam. There is, for example, the alphabet that snakes across the top of the walls, the various accents hanging over the vowels. There are familiar books, which seem beyond the grasp of five-year-olds but which thrill her to see: *Tintin, Les Fables de La Fontaine, Le Petit Prince*. But here the pupils come in varying colours—brown, yellow, and white—though the squealing of children is the same everywhere.

All of this is to be expected. What is surprising is that the teacher does not have a Québécois accent. It is Parisian, like the nuns who raised Josephine. And that accent belongs to a man.

He is very tall and wears a yellow bow tie over a blue sweater vest, both as bright as crayons, and has a five o'clock shadow. He is like Gulliver as he tries to herd the children (dangling from windowsills, buried in plastic toys) to the worn-out polka-dot rug in the centre of the classroom.

Josephine had hoped to simply drop Christian off, but already he is fidgeting with his clip-on tie. She knows he will start wailing the moment she leaves him.

"*Attention*," says the teacher. No response, so he claps his hands. Nothing. He sucks in his breath to let out a holler, then sees Josephine sitting in the corner.

"You're a teacher?" he says.

"No. Not here."

"Oh, I see," he says. "The new boy. You can leave him."

"He will be a nuisance to you if I leave him alone." She says this in French, the first French she has uttered in seven years: "Il sera une nuisance pour vous si je le laisse seul." She is not a smoker, but she can imagine the feeling of a long-awaited relapse. Blood rushes to her head.

Meanwhile the children have stopped in place and now look over at Josephine. She claps her hands. "Over to the front," she says in French.

"I can..." says the teacher, then loses his train of thought as the children gather on the rug at the centre of the classroom for their morning alphabet lesson.

...

The copper statue of General Tran Hung Dao beside Thuong's desk is not the image that most are familiar with — that of Vietnam's great hero who fought off the Mongol invaders almost a millennia before Ho Chi Minh thwarted the French and Americans. It is not the General Tran struck in the tunic, cloak, and shoulder armour of full battle regalia, his dark beard in warring bristle, one finger pointing ahead — to a distant enemy or windswept oasis, Thuong is not sure. In this version, which stands three feet tall, General Tran is dressed as a scholar king. His eyes are just as piercing, but tempered with sympathy. His beard is a pointed wisp. He wears a turban, not his war helmet. His thin cloth belt is wrapped around a scholar's gown that is embroidered with a pattern of clouds. His sword rests in its sheath. In his hand instead is a rolled-up scroll. His victory over the Mongol oppressors is behind him, his fate as a deity lies ahead.

Thuong rescued the statue from the temple in his neighbourhood in Saigon. Who knows what the Communists would have done if they had got their hands on it. Thuong packed it in a huge steamer trunk that belongs to Josephine, swaddled in Josephine's silk dresses.

The statue stands in the corner of the study that doubles as their bedroom, the only spot for it in the basement where all four of them live. When Thuong sits at his desk, he meets the General at eye level on his woodblock pedestal. The statue is still beautiful, although the copper is turning green-blue. Thuong isn't sure whether it is proper to regard the statue as an object of beauty. He is not sure if the look on the General's face is meant to instill awe, or fear, or devotion, or all of these things at once, and if so, in what proportions. This is what he thinks about when he looks upon the General, when he should be working on his dissertation.

Sometimes he thinks the General speaks to him. The General has goaded him to study harder for his exams. He has commanded Thuong to settle on a dissertation topic, even though it may not be the perfect choice. Thuong knows it is improper to pretend that an object of worship would stoop to be his personal academic mentor. But he can't help himself.

Thuong wishes the statue wasn't such a distraction from his studies. Heaven knows, both the university and the Canadian government have given him enough scholarships, stipends, and breaks to get him this far. They have even supplied him with his own IBM PC, which takes up most of his desk, and a daisywheel printer that rocks against the wall when it runs.

But the General is always staring at him, unblinking.

Thuong gets so dizzy sometimes with all his thoughts that he has to stand up, stretch his limbs. Get some fresh air. Call his friend Fred Wong, another economics student. See maybe if there's a card game he can join in Chinatown, just some penny-ante table. Just to take his mind off things.

...

The students call the teacher Monsieur LaForge, though Josephine has learned that his first name is Paul. Against the walls of Paul's classroom are little framed pieces of paper containing pithy quotes in the French language:

> *Happiness is beneficial for the body, but it is grief that develops the powers of the mind.*
> —Marcel Proust

> *Solitary trees, if they grow at all, grow strong.*
> —Winston Churchill

Be less curious about people and more curious about ideas.
   —Marie Curie

Josephine can't help but ask Paul about them.

"They are for the children to read," he says.

"You can't expect them to absorb all this wisdom," says Josephine.

"When I am done, they should at least be able to mouth the words, if not understand them."

Josephine has attended the half-day kindergarten all week. Christian starts crying even if she gets up to go to the washroom, and has not improved.

Paul was at first annoyed by Josephine's presence. It was one thing for five-year-olds to judge him, it was another thing to have an adult's eyes on him as well. But Paul cannot deny the calming effect that Josephine has on all the children. When she is not in the room, they not only fidget, as five-year-olds do, but cough, go glassy-eyed, snap at each other, nod off, make a break for the Lego. Perhaps it has to do with Paul's deep, sonorous voice delivered at the pace of a metronome, a voice that could command the attention of a jury but which lies outside the register of young children. Josephine just barks across the room when there's defiance. She has a tone that corrals the children when they lose their focus on Paul.

It is during a rendition of "Ballade à la lune," when the children start laughing in the middle of the song, that Paul can smell sulphur. The children pinch their noses, then point fingers at each other, and then the fingers settle on a little red-headed girl with a sombre expression. The smell gathers strength. As the girl's pallor turns pink and tears roll down her face, the children laugh harder and clear a radius around her.

Josephine comes to the girl, checks under her navy dress, and picks her up by the armpits.

"It's diarrhea," says Josephine.

"Oh dear," says Paul.

"I'll take her to the washroom. Can you bring a pair of pants?"

"How would I have an extra pair of pants?"

"The nuns must have supplies," says Josephine. "You must have a physical education department? An extra pair of shorts or jogging pants in a locker room? It doesn't have to be the perfect size."

"Of course," says Paul. "I'll be right back."

Paul does not realize that he has sweated through his dress shirt until class is done. The red-headed girl's mother shudders when she finds her daughter in baggy sweatpants.

"She had an accident," says Paul.

"You changed her?" says the mother accusingly. She hisses in relief when Paul points at Josephine.

Josephine stays after all the other children have gone, waiting for Christian, who is so absorbed with a strange-looking toy that she finally has to pull it away.

"Until tomorrow," she says.

"You know, I really teach fourth grade," says Paul. "Fourth grade and up."

"I understand."

"I'm just substituting for the term," says Paul. "Until a spot opens up in fourth grade. Or higher. Hopefully."

"We will see you tomorrow."

"Certainly."

...

Thuong's daydreams are as vivid as his nighttime visions. Now he is on a warship, looking for General Tran. The year is 1288. The Mongol naval fleet has settled at the mouth of the Bach Dang River, close to Hanoi.

Under General Tran's direction, the Vietnamese navy waits until high tide, and then its fleet engages the enemy's boats. When the tide ebbs, the Vietnamese boats retreat towards the ocean. The Mongol boats give chase, not realizing that the Vietnamese have laid metal spikes along the riverbed. The Mongols' heavier, sturdier boats become embedded in the spikes in low tide. Meanwhile, another cohort of the Vietnamese fleet have been lying in wait in the tributaries behind the Mongol boats. The Mongols are surrounded and skewered.

Thuong is on the deck of a ship, but General Tran is nowhere in view. In fact, Thuong is among the Mongols, tall, burly, bearded men wearing looks of horror. They see through him, run right through him. The ship is sinking. In the distance he can hear the victory chants of his countrymen, while the Mongols around him are helplessly bailing out water with giant clamshells.

...

Once a year, on Josephine's birthday, Thuong cuts her hair outside in the old style. Not only is it his tradition to do it outdoors, but there is no room in the basement to properly cut hair. Outside there is an old apple tree, its protruding roots radiating through the backyard. There is a nail on the tree where Thuong hangs up a mirror in a frame. There is a fold-out wooden reclining chair and a small plastic table where he lays out his implements. Thuong does his barbering bare-chested, so that he does not defile a good shirt with her hair. He keeps a folded white towel over one shoulder.

It is unfortunate that Josephine's birthday is at the end of September, when, in Vancouver, the sunlight is spotty at best. At least today it's not raining. In the afternoon Josephine has set out *banh uot* in the kitchen when Thuong calls her outside. She knows what is coming. "I don't need a haircut," she says through the window, as she always does, and as always, Thuong leads her outside, her arm held in his arm, after Josephine has put on her blue-laced slippers to walk on the moist grass.

He ignores his mother, who croaks out the window, "Leave her alone."

Josephine wears her hair long and straight, cascading over her shoulders. Every year he takes off five inches.

"You know this is my true calling," says Thuong, who is the son of a barber. "You thought you were going to marry a professor."

"I thought I was going to marry a colonel." They regard each other through the mirror, the one time in the whole year they make eye contact while talking. "I can settle for a professor," she says.

Every year, Thuong thinks, Josephine becomes more beautiful. Every year, it becomes harder to hold her gaze.

"Wait," says Thuong. He calls Christian out from the basement. "Get the sprayer." Christian mists Josephine's hair while Thuong pulls out the scissors from their plastic cover.

Next door is a barking Doberman. Around dinnertime it sticks its nose through the wooden fence posts and snarls at the apple tree. Now it is digging into one of the posts to loosen the soil around it. The dog's Cantonese owners have complained to Thuong's landlord, although it's been months since Christian threw fallen apples at the dog. Thuong's mother speculates it's Josephine's cooking that sets the dog off. The dog gets this way no matter the dish, whether it's beef noodle soup, imperial rolls, or even her cold shrimp and papaya salad.

The barking usually doesn't bother Thuong, but now he nicks his little finger with the scissors.

"I'm fine."

"You've lost your focus," says Josephine. "Maybe it's the new incense." She means the joss sticks that he burns for his father's altar in their bedroom, the ones he got from Chinatown. "It keeps me awake too. It smells impure."

"There's nothing wrong with the incense."

"They are opening up a temple on Kingsway," she says. "You should get some proper joss sticks there."

"A temple in Vancouver? Buddhist? Vietnamese?"

"I think so. You should also take that statue of yours. Leave it with the monks. You've been distracted by it. I can tell."

"No, I haven't."

Josephine never complained when Thuong asked her to stow the statue in her trunk, never mentioned all the dresses she gave up, the farewell presents from her students that she had to leave behind. She had thought the statue was struck in pure gold, and was shocked when Thuong rubbed off the gold paint so it wouldn't be confiscated by the border guards. She thought Thuong salvaged the icon for love of country, so there would be one less treasure the Communists could get their hands on. She didn't think Thuong actually worshipped the folk deity. After all, Thuong got baptized just before they got married. They go to church every Sunday.

"Why else can't you get your degree?"

Thuong taps her cheek with the scissors. "Please don't," he says. "Not today."

Josephine brushes the scissors off her face. "Does the General belong in a temple or in our bedroom?" she says. They stare at each other through the mirror.

It takes all of Thuong's power to peel his eyes away from her. When he is done cutting, he takes the towel and wipes her hair off his chest. The dog will not stop barking.

"Fish sauce," yells Thuong's mother through the window. "That's what makes the dog crazy." Fish sauce is the common ingredient in every dish Josephine makes.

...

There is one framed quotation Josephine had not noticed until today's class, because it hangs in the corner where the children are sent to be punished: "*La vérité, comme la lumière, aveugle.*"

The truth, like the light, makes one blind. By Camus.

She cannot focus during class. This is the guilt that Josephine cannot admit to: she has read *L'Étranger* more times than any other book, except perhaps the Bible. There is little that moves her, but she cannot keep her eyes from moistening when the protagonist Meursault drinks coffee idly in front of his mother's coffin. Nothing, nothing in the great Vietnamese romantic fables touches her as much as when, at Meursault's trial, he can only blame the sun for his shooting the motionless Arab those four times. Nothing even in the Book of Exodus moves her as when Meursault is asked if he loved his mother, and he answers yes, the same as anyone.

She cannot explain it. She is as much an existentialist as the crucifix she wears is made out of water.

Maybe she feels all the things Meursault is unable to.

Each scene of the novel evokes in her the true Christian feelings that Meursault ought to have if he were Christian as well. Plus there is the added pity she feels for Camus, for only a writer who feels such sorrow for the world can create a figure of such tragic emptiness. And yet she cannot condemn Meaursault. She comes back to the novel at least once a year, not truly convinced there is no place in paradise for such a man.

After class she tells Paul that *L'Étranger* is her favourite novel. She has never admitted this to anyone. Paul wipes his face wearily, as if every one of his students has told him this.

"It's mine too," he says.

"But you must love God?"

"I do."

"Then isn't it difficult to reconcile?" she says.

"It is very difficult," he says, with furrowed eyebrows. "But we have to try, don't we? Even if we have to start over every day."

...

Josephine really does have a magic touch with the children. Those who fall off their plastic chairs, or scrape their knees during recess, go to Josephine for ministrations. Paul is free to concentrate on his lesson.

Josephine's presence is based on a fib, and the fib is different depending on who you ask. The nuns are told that Christian will break into tears and wet himself if

Josephine leaves him for even a moment. The parents are told that she is a teacher in training. The children are told, for a laugh, that she is Gulliver's wife.

...

Among the toys is one the children don't know what to do with. It is the size of a tennis ball, but it doesn't bounce. Josephine cannot tell them what it is. She shows it to Paul.

"It's a heart," he says.

"It looks deformed."

"No. It's the real thing, more or less." It's a model of a five-year-old's heart, for medical school. The object looks like a toy, with the aorta, veins, and arteries rendered in a brightly coloured plastic.

Some child fished it out from Paul's top desk drawer. It belonged to Paul's late father, once the chief of surgery at Sainte-Justine Hospital in Montreal. His specialty was mending the hearts of babies and little children. If you were a young child in Montreal during the 1960s, and if you had heart troubles, then the chances were good that you knew Paul's father. He also taught in academies in Lyon and Paris, where Paul spent his childhood summers. Paul never thought of his accent as Parisian, but if Josephine thinks so, then this was how he picked it up.

Paul became an engineer. If he had become a doctor, he would merely be a sparrow walking in the footprints of a bear. He thought he would actually design things the world had never seen, which was better than what his father did. For what was a surgeon but a glorified mechanic, simply maintaining the designs of a greater creator?

Nobody told Paul when he dreamed of designing bridges that he would end up stamping drawings for retaining walls in residential subdivisions. Nobody told him that the materials of his trade would be modest lengths of Allan Block and shotcrete sprayed on boulder stone, not miles of big bright steel.

If only he saw the potential of retaining walls, these seemingly modest structures. Because something small can fail just as spectacularly as something big. Nobody told Paul this either.

The day he quit engineering was the day his father died, and he left Montreal soon after. If asked why he would want to trade Montreal for Vancouver, the Canadiens for the Canucks, Paul will never mention all the strangers he met in Montreal whose first question to him was whether he was his father's son. He will never mention the last straw, that woman he picked up at a bar in the Old Quarter, that night in his apartment when, in tearful gratitude, she lifted the floating edge of her left breast to show Paul the scar that his father had left on her as a child. He will not speak of the odd satisfaction he gets for being paid in Vancouver to teach something that he never really had to learn.

And anyway, he still keeps his Canadiens key chain.

...

The statue of General Tran is hollow. Thuong could have carried it himself down Fleming Street to the bus stop on Kingsway, but he got Christian to help him. It is time for the boy to taste labour.

Thuong and the boy carry the statue outside with the General gazing skyward. The boy has the General by his heels while Thuong cradles his upper shoulders with his palms. The boy has to walk backwards. As soon as Christian turns his head so that he can see the way ahead, Thuong stops.

"Don't lose your focus," says Thuong. "Keep your eyes on me."

Neighbours stare from their yards as the pair take delicate steps down the sidewalk. Thuong has walked this path many times before, but now it feels much longer. He starts to count the number of blocks.

Sweat forms around the boy's temples. It's his mother's fault, putting so many layers of clothes on him. "Don't you dare drop it," says Thuong, and the boy nods. Four blocks, five blocks, six, and he sees the sweat come down the boy's face. Or is it tears?

At the bus stop, they set the General back on his feet. Thuong strokes his son's ear. "Well done," he says, just in time to see the bus with the twin sparkles of its BC Hydro livery.

They get off after only a couple of stops. The outside of the temple looks like an autobody shop, with its corrugated siding and flat rooftop. The inside smells otherworldly, but what Thuong first thinks is incense is actually plaster dust. The space was used briefly as a tae kwon do dojo, but the business was unprofitable. The lowered rents have provided an opportunity for the Vietnamese community's first Buddhist temple.

The abbot greets Thuong with a hug. "We're still renovating," he says.

"It's already better than gathering to pray in someone's basement."

The monk laughs. "It has been too long," he says. "Are you here for a favour or a blessing?"

"Not a favour, but I could always use a blessing. I am here to make you an offering. General Tran Hung Dao."

"That is a gift no man can give."

Thuong takes the monk outside, where Christian is guarding the statue. The General looks no more out of place on this intersection with its gas stations than the monk in saffron robes.

"You'll agree he is entitled to a more suitable venue than my study."

"But we are making a house for Lord Buddha," says the monk.

"Of course. The General won't usurp Buddha. Perhaps give General Tran a small space for people who want to make him an offering as well. You'll get more visitors."

The monk shuffles his sandals. "If we let the General in, then who's next? We'll open a floodgate to more statues of deities."

"You shouldn't worry."

"This is to be a serious place of contemplation and enlightenment."

"Of course."

"I don't want it to become a place where men go to make offerings to get rich, or where women go to light incense to get pregnant."

"It shouldn't come to that," says Thuong. "Besides, it's the deity Me Sanh that the women pray to in order to get pregnant, not Tran Hung Dao."

"I suppose you'd want a share of the offerings," says the monk.

This makes Thuong smile. "I could always use a blessing."

The monk agrees to reserve a small space for General Tran, perhaps near the front door to ward off evil spirits. Before leaving, he gives Thuong a box of joss sticks made out of the best aloeswood from their homeland. Josephine should be relieved.

It is turning out to be a fine afternoon, and so Thuong walks home the whole way, carrying Christian on his shoulders.

...

"What would you do without me?" says Josephine. Today she has untangled two girls fighting over a toy, consoled another boy, wiped another tear, kissed another bruise, plugged, once again, the floodgate of hell.

"I don't know," says Paul.

"Maybe you can pay me a salary."

Paul smiles. "As if that was possible."

"Then private lessons, for my son?"

Paul nods. He has noticed how much further Christian has advanced than the other children. Josephine has been tutoring Christian at home. While the others are still learning single words, Christian is already making sentences with properly conjugated verbs.

"You're a teacher too," says Paul. "What could I offer?"

"Your voice," she says. "Your Parisian accent. Not my Vietnamese French."

"Your accent is fine," he says, but puts up only weak resistance.

Paul takes from his desk Goscinny and Sempé's *Le Petit Nicolas*. They find a booth in a White Spot down the street. Josephine orders all three of them mushroom burgers even though Paul didn't ask for one. He has a sandwich at home. But when he smells the mushrooms, he is silently grateful for it.

Paul gets Christian to read the Goscinny. He has heard Christian's voice rise above the others during class, but has never heard it alone in close quarters. Although Paul cannot take credit for the boy's sudden grasp of the language, he can hear in Christian faint echoes of his own street *joual*, something he has been trying to purge since his first summer in Paris, the way he still runs his words together. Christian's voice is also layered with a wavering musicality — the Vietnamese accent that

Josephine has imparted to her son and now wants to get rid of.

"He reads beautifully," says Paul.

"Then it's something worth working on?" says Josephine. Paul nods, and Josephine sees the little frayed threads on Paul's collared shirt. If only she had the money, she would buy Paul a new one.

...

The Doberman breaks through the wooden fence while Josephine is picking mint leaves in the backyard. The landlord forbids any garden, but has not noticed the mint grove that she planted. The dog heads straight for Josephine, who is on her knees with her back turned. She does not register the Doppler effect of the oncoming muzzle.

Thuong gets in the way just before the dog lunges. She has no idea where Thuong came from, but that's nothing new. He slams his thin bare arm lengthwise between the dog's open jaws, like a crowbar, to the back of the dog's mouth. The dog's teeth drip saliva, then blood. No longer barking, it wheezes like a broken flute and retreats back through the gap in the fence.

"Your arm."

"It's nothing," says Thuong. "It's the dog's blood. I broke its jaw." Still, there are teeth marks on Thuong's arm that Josephine has to clean up. The noodles she made are now waterlogged, wasted.

The problem is not Thuong's loyalty but his wisdom in exercising it. Like when Josephine had heard a loud clapping and climbed up to the rooftop of her school in Saigon to survey what seemed like a thunderstorm in the middle of a sunny day—the quiet hush of a single blue-and-white Renault taxi coasting past the line of baby palm trees on the street below, the orange-tiled roofs of the villas dotting the neighbourhood, and the blue sky in the far distance turning grey from crackling storm clouds of smoke. She had been up there so long, standing in the dizzying sunshine and mesmerized by the firefight on the outskirts of the city, that Thuong went after her and carried her back down, thinking she was going to jump off. On the last flight of stairs he tripped and they both fell. He broke her fall and his arm in the process.

Or the time he came home with a broken thumb. He said he had just won them a flight to Hong Kong on a diplomatic carrier by beating a colonel at cards. Later, Josephine was told by Thuong not to pay attention to the rumours that he had shot a private because the colonel had ordered him to, and was sent away to shut him up. "Don't question fortune," Thuong said. He never explained how he broke his thumb.

Or that night in Hong Kong when Thuong had a crisis of conscience and jumped into the harbour to swim back to Vietnam to fight for his country. The Hong Kong Marine Police fished him out and found nothing on him except for his toothbrush and a wallet with Josephine's picture.

...

It has become routine for them to convene after school at the White Spot. Paul looks forward to the post-classroom calm of listening to Christian's lone voice as he reads, and to helping prune the boy's voice to its sharper, truer self.

On this day they do not meet after class. Josephine has to take Christian to the dentist. Paul, though, insists that they continue the lesson later in the day, so that Christian will not lose his momentum. In the meantime Paul naps in his studio apartment. He does not feel like pulling out the mattress, so he sleeps on the couch, surrounded by posters and knick-knacks acquired from all the places he has been to: a Monet print from the Louvre, sand in a bottle from Mauritius, replica Lewis chessmen from London. Paul had travelled mostly with his father. He hasn't done much since. Just hasn't had the time, or otherwise hasn't been able to afford it.

The three of them meet, this time, in the late afternoon. Paul wears a freshly ironed shirt. She wears, for the first time, lipstick. Christian seems more withdrawn. Everyone acts more gingerly around each other. It has to do with the break after the class, the change in the angle of sunlight.

Yet she can ask questions that she would not during the day. Like: "Are you a Roman Catholic?"

"Yes," says Paul, which is not a lie, because he was baptized.

"Which church do you attend?"

"The one at school, sometimes," he says, which is a lie.

"We usually go to St. Joseph's, but we'll try the school's. Then we'll see you this Sunday?"

"Sure," says Paul, then steers them back to the lesson. He pulls out from his vest pocket his paperback version of *L'Étranger*. "Christian can read from this."

"Oh no," says Josephine. Paul has never seen her blush before.

"I'm sorry. I didn't mean anything. Maybe he's too young."

Josephine takes a deep breath and smiles. "That's fine," she says. "He can try."

Christian puts his fingers on the page as if trying to find the words by touch. To help him along, Josephine reads: "Aujourd'hui, maman est morte. Ou peut-être hier, je ne sais pas." She is more uncomfortable reading French out loud than just speaking it herself, feels that her instrument is too blunt for Camus's words, that she is tone-deaf to his music. Paul nods and smiles. Christian repeats his mother's words. Under Paul's forgiving gaze, Josephine finds it in her to continue to read and to wait for her son's echo.

They read until she looks up at the clock and gasps. "I'm late for work."

"You work at night?"

"Yes, downtown. I have to take Christian home first."

"I can take him," says Paul.

"Are you sure?"

"No problem. Is someone at home?"

"His father and grandmother."

"Okay then."

Josephine darts off. Later, Christian leads Paul down Fleming Street, keeping two steps ahead, past stucco houses and wooden hydro poles. Paul sings "Ballade à la lune" to cut the silence. An oncoming car has its high beams on, narrowing his pupils, and when he adjusts to the night again, Christian is gone.

Christian must have turned the corner into a side alley. Paul starts running. When he reaches the next turn to the back alley, he sees Christian pumping his legs beneath the lamplight. He catches up, puts a hand on Christian's shoulder. They are both panting.

"This isn't a game," says Paul.

"This is my home," says Christian. Paul follows him down concrete stairs to the back door. Thuong answers the door wearing an unfortunate wife-beater. He has to crane his neck to meet Paul eye to eye.

"Did Tommy send you?" says Thuong, then notices Christian. "Where did you find him?"

"I'm his French teacher," says Paul.

Thuong smiles. "I'm a teacher too. Well, almost. I study economics."

Thuong rubs the dressing on his arm. His eyes are red and slightly bulging, and Paul thinks at first that Thuong is drunk, but his stare is too steady and lucid. With the look of murder, but lucid.

"How is my son doing?"

"He's wonderful."

"I'm so relieved," says Thuong. "A good teacher is so important in a young man's life."

"I agree," says Paul.

Thuong seems to be staring at Paul's forehead, maybe trying to look him in the eyes.

"You need a haircut," says Thuong, "and a shave."

Paul brushes the back of his scruffy head. "Maybe so."

"Commanding respect begins with a good haircut and a close shave."

"You're right."

"Stay for tea."

"Thank you, but no," says Paul. He heads back to the alleyway.

...

Josephine works at the top of a thirty-storey building. Or at least that is where she starts, before making her way down one storey at a time, in her cleaner's uniform and cart with the dual mop bucket. Her luxury is a silk handkerchief that she wraps around her face, the same one that shielded her from the sun in Saigon, and which now spares her from dust.

The top floors are occupied by a law firm with varnished rosewood offices, its founders memorialized in oils hung on the walls. These offices are more lavishly appointed than any church she knows, yet they fall short of achieving the grace to which the firm no doubt aspires.

She lingers at a wall-length window facing north. She rests her chin on her mop, eye level with the lighted ski slopes of Grouse Mountain. She has not been in a building this tall since she was in Hong Kong, where she saw the New Year's fireworks. Gaudy dragons lighting up the night, which reminded her of the firefight she saw on that rooftop in Saigon.

Up here her mind lingers on Paul and her son together, Paul's voice, his freckled hands around *L'Étranger*. There is no way that heaven can be located in the sky, with what she has seen from this vantage point, considering what she thinks of when she is up this high.

...

Professor Jennings calls Thuong into his office overlooking the North Shore Mountains, tells Thuong that his efforts to debunk Communist economics based on his application of game theory simply cannot be defended.

"I'll try again," says Thuong. "Another hypothesis."

"There's no point," says Jennings. "It's been five years. You're brilliant, in your own way, but you aren't meant for economics. I'm sorry it's taken so long to realize this. That is the department's failing."

"I'll do anything," says Thuong.

By the time they are finished, both men are shaken. Thuong stares at the ground all the way to the bus stop. He will not head home. Not straight away. Somewhere is a card game to take his mind off things. Just penny-ante fare.

...

On Sunday morning, Josephine wakes up alone in bed, thinking that Thuong has been spirited away. When she gets up to look for him, opens the back door, and sees what stands before her, she does not hear herself shriek, does not feel her heels leave the ground as she trips over the loose threshold, her chin landing on a clay pot on the concrete step.

Outside stands the General. His expression, Josephine has finally decided, is of someone betrayed.

Thuong, as always, appears out of nowhere. "You're bleeding," he says. He pulls her off the floor. "You need a bandage."

"Why is he back?" she says. "I thought he had come for me."

"You have a guilty conscience."

"That's not an answer." Josephine goes into the kitchen for a white towel, which she presses to her chin.

"I went to the temple. I found him in storage. The monks never intended to give him an altar."

"What were you doing at the temple?"

"Praying."

"To whom?"

Thuong ignores her question. "I couldn't leave him there," he says. He carries the statue back to its corner.

"Wake up Christian. We should get ready for church."

"Go without me."

"Why?"

He smiles apologetically. "I have to study."

Josephine and Christian walk to St. Maurice's under cloud cover. Its church has no bells to greet the parishioners, no steps to ascend to the nave. The service is in English and so Josephine has difficulty understanding much of it. Paul arrives during the Universal Prayer in his Sunday best—a pair of navy-blue dress pants and a blazer, an orange bow tie with navy-blue polka dots— although he is shaggy around the ears and sporting a two-week growth on his face. He kneels beside her. He hasn't knelt since he was a child. When they drop their chins in prayer, he feels as though they are play-acting. Before the prayer is over, Paul cheats, opens his eyes, and takes in Josephine's profile while her eyes are closed. Her expression is beatific from this angle. He does not notice the welt on her chin until she turns her head.

"What happened to you?"

"Just an accident," she says. The blood has dried, but the bruise on her chin is still blooming.

"Your husband did this?"

"I fell."

"Let me see." Paul cannot help but touch her. It is the first time he has done so, two fingers on the boundary between white skin and violet. He tilts her bruise up like a jewel to the dim, yellow stained-glass light. It is a perfect oval. Nothing shaped so precisely can be by accident.

In the pews they wish peace on their neighbours, many of whom are familiar children from the school and their parents, who smile among themselves, as if confirming a truth about Paul and Josephine that they have always known. Then they walk up together to receive Communion, while Christian receives a blessing.

After Mass, Paul offers to walk them home and eventually Josephine relents. Paul has one hand on Christian's shoulder and the other in a fist. Josephine walks by Paul's side. They take their sweet time in the Vancouver sunlight, which shines as shyly as they do.

When they reach her backyard, they cannot see to the house because the clothesline from the apple tree to the fence is thick with her laundry, clothes that from afar look like dead birds strung upside down. Crows and pigeons, blue birds and red robins, seagulls and doves. Thuong has never done the laundry before.

There is the smell of lunch in the air. Thuong stands behind the clothesline. His shirt is off, his ribs are rack thin. He is urinating on Josephine's mint.

"Do you want me to talk to him?" says Paul to Josephine. She ignores him.

"What are you doing?" she says to Thuong.

"Fertilizing," says Thuong. He turns, zips up his khaki pants, and walks right up to Paul. "Eat with us," he says.

"I don't know," says Paul, but before he can finish his thought, Thuong and Christian bring out the fold-out table. Then they bring out chairs—some wooden, some plastic.

"You might as well," says Josephine.

Banh uot, vermicelli noodles, and prawns with their eyes still attached are doled out on paper plates by

Thuong and his mother. "We save them for special occasions," says Thuong of the plates and plastic cutlery. The five of them sit around the table and, after Josephine says grace, they eat in silence. Paul has never tried Vietnamese food. His nostrils flare when he smells the fish sauce. The food feels strange when it touches his lips, never mind his tongue. The *banh uot* has a rubbery consistency, and he is not sure if the filling is a ground meat or vegetable paste.

Thuong brings out a six-pack of Molson Canadian. "A friend gave me this gift, but I just keep it under our bed." Thuong pours his beer into a glass full of ice. Paul would rather drink warm beer straight from the can. The fish sauce makes him thirsty and when he finishes one beer he accepts another. When the old lady offers Paul another helping of *banh uot*, he does not refuse. He did not know how hungry he is.

"I was supposed to be a teacher," Thuong says. "But I was really meant to cut hair."

"Being a teacher is so hard," says Paul.

Josephine pecks at her food and looks at the line of hanging clothes as if at any moment they will fly away. Christian doesn't want the day to end because when he sleeps, he always dreams his mother is missing. No one can protect her except for him.

When all the food and beer are gone, Thuong says something in Vietnamese and Christian gets up to clear the table. Thuong nudges Paul to get off his seat so he can put it away.

"Now, since you're my guest, you should let me cut your hair," says Thuong.

"No, that's okay," says Paul. He feels drowsy when he stands up.

"I insist," Thuong says. Then in Vietnamese he says: "I need the practice. That's my price if you want to take my family."

"You're being crazy," says Josephine.

"Am I?" says Thuong.

"What are you all saying?" says Paul.

"Now that he is on my property, he can't just leave," says Thuong.

Josephine throws her hands up in the air and pulls out the reclining chair herself. "Have it your way," she says.

"What's going on?" says Paul.

Josephine turns to him. "The sooner you do this, the sooner we can move on," she says in French. "Trust me."

Paul thinks about his dead father and realizes that Josephine is the only one left in this world he does trust.

"I don't understand you," says Thuong.

"You don't have to," says Josephine.

Paul sits on the chair under the apple tree. Thuong barks something at Christian, who goes to fetch a white towel and scissors. The mirror is already hung against the tree. The sprayer is at the ready on the lampstand. The old lady is by the window, telling Thuong to leave the tall man alone. Thuong says something that makes her disappear from the windowsill.

Thuong gets Paul to remove his blazer, uses a piece of a Glad garbage bag as a cutting cape, and starts snipping away. "Why is kindergarten your profession?" says Thuong.

"I didn't choose it," says Paul. "I'm waiting to teach older children."

Thuong puts a hand on Paul's shoulder. "A man becoming something is just as good as a man who already is something."

Paul nods, though he doesn't really get it. Or maybe at some level he does get it, because all of a sudden he feels a little bit better about things.

Something about how Thuong turns the steel scissors into a butterfly, fluttering in the back, around the ears, an inch off the top, soothes Paul. When Thuong is done, he gives Paul a hand mirror, walks around Paul with the larger portrait mirror to show off his handiwork.

"It's perfect," says Paul. "Maybe you are on to something."

"I'm not done," says Thuong. He tilts the chair back so that Paul is facing the apple blossoms above. "You need a shave."

"I don't know," says Paul, but Thuong has, from somewhere, pulled out a brush and jar of shaving cream. Josephine is nowhere in sight.

"Relax," says Thuong. "I'm going to give you a real man's shave."

Thuong applies the cream to Paul's beard. His son comes out with a paddle strop and a towel that Thuong's mother has steamed in a pot. The steaming towel that Thuong wraps around Paul's face is like a narcotic, and Paul almost falls asleep. When the towel is removed and Paul sees the straight razor in Thuong's hand, dripping sunlight, he does not panic. Maybe it's because his father used one, and taught Paul how to use it as well. Paul just closes his eyes, feels the razor brush against his cheeks, down to his Adam's apple, and gives himself to fate.

When Thuong is done, he calls Josephine out, to show her his true talent, as much as to show Paul's face, unmasked, so that there is nothing for anyone to hide.

The Tale of Jude

Lee will never forget his first bus ride to St. Crispin's School, getting picked up on Sargent Avenue in Winnipeg's West End, so early in the morning. The opening bell will not ring for another hour and a half. The approaching school bus gleams like a silver ghost, the only creature on the road at this hour. He is the first passenger. The bus picks up no other passenger until it is well south of his neighbourhood, past the dilapidated clapboard houses that in any other city would be given a heritage designation, would be snapped up by yuppies and restored to a sheen. Houses bunched up together, even though there is plenty of land here to spread out. The only way you could tell whether a house was lived in or abandoned was if the yard was overgrown with weeds or if the grass was mown down to a burnt yellow brush cut.

The bus fills up one by one, boys at various stages of puberty, in red blazers or black leather varsity jackets, carrying backpacks or briefcases or bulky hockey bags. The bus turns off of Pembina Highway towards the Drive. Lee leans towards the window and the immense riverside homes like a plant leans towards the sun. The houses get bigger the closer he gets to the school. It has been a hot, dry summer, but the lawns here are so lush it is as if Lee has travelled not to another neighbourhood but to another clime.

He expects to enter the school through massive wrought-iron gates, but there is only a wooden sign. The school has no need for a gate. The surrounding neighbourhood, the forbidding display of suburban wealth, is the school's only necessary defence.

On one side of the grounds is a giant green field, multiple soccer pitches laid side by side, bordered by pine trees, fields where you can kick the ball as hard as you want without worry of hitting the road. On the other side are the school buildings, modern brick extravagances with large glass facades, like an institute of technology both vintage and modern. Tucked away from these buildings, closer to the riverbank, is a smaller, old brick mansion, with a single vine of ivy running along its side, like a raised vein, and a porte cochère attached for ghost buggies.

Lee is the first one on the bus, last one out. He walks with his spine bent to his first class, following the orientation arrows. Before the first day has started, he already knows which of the boys he will tangle with before year's end.

...

He will take to heart none of the school traditions. Not the morning assembly of the Upper School, with hockey players and science geeks breaking out in unison to sing William Blake's "Jerusalem," the sea of red wool blazers and the subtle variations between them, the differently striped house ties, the debating pins on a few of the lapels, the absence of them on the others, the geometric billowing of the double Windsor knots worn by the prefects, the brute single Windsors worn by the rest. Not the strange games played during phys. ed.: lacrosse, rugby, ultimate Frisbee, capture the flag. Not the lunches on long oak tables under the plaques of winners of the various mathematics contests — the Cayley, Pascal, and Fermat. Not ham sandwiches beneath engraved names. Not the honours and stripes recorded in the school diaries.

He will take home none of this as he changes into his jeans and T-shirt for the bus ride home. T-shirts that show off his biceps hung on a slim frame, like rats on a spit.

When he gets home, he goes to the back of their clapboard house, to the entrance of the basement suite, where he and his mother live. He knocks on the door, even though he has a key, because he never knows whether his mother is alone. Mondays are supposed to be his mother's night off, so Lee expects to find her either napping or with company. But she is sitting alone at the kitchen table, dressed in her waitress uniform for tonight's extra shift. Skirt, name tag, apron. She has worn the same skirt for years, but Lee is reaching an age when he is starting to think that it is too short.

She is counting her tips from the night before. Mounds of loose change. She hates these loonies, which the mint introduced just last year. Usually she changes her tips into bills, but last night she carried all of her change home in the front of her apron.

Dangling from her neck is a gold necklace anchored by a jade ring, like a green lifesaver. Lee has never seen it before. With his mother's wage and tips she has kept a roof over Lee's head and his belly full, but her money does not account for their sixteen-inch colour TV and VHS recorder, the stereo system in Lee's room, the silk dresses in her closet, her Passat.

His mother is stacking the coins into towers of loonies, quarters, dimes, and nickels. "I want to see what my day was worth," she says. "I think the tips are bigger during the day than at night. To think I've been working nights all this time."

"It probably doesn't make much of a difference," he says, meaning his words as consolation.

His mother puts her fingers on one stack then another, like a chess player unsure what her move is. "You lost my count," she says.

"Fifty-seven dollars and thirty-five cents," says Lee. Both Lee and his mother know that Lee is right to the nickel. Bored once, he figured out the thickness of each type of coin. His mother, on the other hand, can't keep numbers in her head. Lee has no idea where he got this gift.

Dinner is on the stove, and he eats his lemon grass chicken with the plate on his knees while he pores over his brand new analytic geometry text. He will take nothing to heart from his Latin, ancient history, or even his chemistry class. He is at the school for one reason alone: mathematics.

...

There are no girls on his bus, though Lee was told during his entrance interview that the Upper School had recently become coed. In his grade ten class consisting of over eighty students, there are only five girls. He did not spot one until mid-week.

Two of the girls, Tracy Felton and Chelsea Dubinsky, are reputedly to die for. In the locker room Lee can barely concentrate on getting out of his charcoal-grey pants and into jeans with the hockey players shouting over each other, laying claim to them. One of the girls is a studious Asian. Another one, Sofia Orlofsky, seems too cool for this school. The last girl is named Jude. Lee knows nothing about her other than that, for some reason, she has attracted the boys' mockery and ire. The boys call her La Vache—the Cow—possibly because she is tall and big-boned.

*Moo*s follow Jude wherever she goes. *Moo*s take on the quality of water, seep through classroom walls and nip at her heels down hallways and in the dining hall and even outside, male cackles like raindrops off the leaves of the campus fruit trees. They moo everywhere except in the computer room.

...

The computer room at St. Crispin's is an altogether different place. It is called the Dunster Computer Room, after one of the school's many esteemed benefactors. The room is the size of a basketball half court on an upper floor, appearing to the outsider to be floating in the air, row upon row of computer screens flickering through tall glass.

The only adornment in the computer room is a large Chinese hand scroll of a lonely, willowy tree hanging over a misty mountainside, framed in an expensive-looking light wood. Lee expects that the landscape is there as a lesson of some sort, but Mr. Wharton, the teacher, never alludes to it.

The computers are the latest desktops from Compaq. The class is an introduction to programming in Pascal. Lee, to his surprise, is hooked. His first assignment is simple: make a program that draws a happy face. When he tries, the program simply won't run and reports syntax errors. The screen remains blank. When he finally gets the program to run, a blinking green circle forms on the screen, but it freezes before an expression appears. He has made drawing a happy face into something complicated, like baking a soufflé that keeps toppling over. His code writing becomes ever more overgrown. But when he does succeed, when the happy face stares back at him, it feels to him truly a live thing.

The students here are different from those in other classes. Computer science is an elective, which eliminates all the jocks. There is a pressure to get to know each other here more than anywhere else. Everyone in computer class chose to be in computer class, and therefore chose each other, in a way. Chosen ones can't just ignore each other. Lee can ignore geeks in math, but here he has to learn their names.

Everyone talks to everyone, that is, except to the girl Jude, who sits in the back row where the computers are in sleep mode. Jude, who has attracted the enmity of the boys in the school's wider world — the jocks and the hand-pressing prefects who try to ingratiate themselves with the jocks — has found asylum here. Here, she is ignored, but not because she is despised. To the computerists she is a woman, and therefore a unicorn. They feel uncomfortable with her the way you would with jewellery in an unsecured room. Every so often they look sideways to see if she is still around. But they can't speak to her. There is a sound barrier between them and Jude that they can't break.

...

When Lee lifts his head from the fountain, it is Jude who is standing behind him. "You missed a spot," she says, pointing to the spot under his chin where a hockey player's fist had left a ripe plum.

"I wasn't washing my face," says Lee.

"It stings just looking at it."

"Try wearing it," says Lee.

"I have."

...

The next challenge in computer class is to create a billiards program, something that plays eight ball and cutthroat. Lee can't make his program work. The balls bounce off each other at angles that defy the laws of nature. The other students are already done. Lee stays behind after the bell to work out the bugs. He stays as long as necessary. He misses the bus. He will walk home, even if it takes him all night.

"Let me see."

He turns around. The girl Jude has been sitting behind him all along.

"You're not done either?"

"Just polishing up. Tell me what you think." Her pool game hums like a Cadillac. The balls go where they should. She's also added the possibility of putting English on the cue ball and various aesthetic embellishments — enamelling on the cues, glinting balls reflecting the light bulbs above the table, oak varnish on the side panels. Jude could package this program for Nintendo.

"Let me see yours." Before Lee can do anything, like kick in his computer screen, she is already running his program.

"Let me see the code," she says. Lee draws it up on the screen. She squints at his program, scrolling down with excruciating patience. "The program is as long as mine," she says. "It doesn't have to be. May I?"

Before he can deny her, her large, thick fingers flutter over the keyboard as if she is doing fine needlework, but when he looks at what she has done on the screen, it is clear she has conducted major surgery. His code has been sawed down to its essence. It reads elegantly and runs without bugs.

"Thanks," he says. "See you tomorrow."

It is pitch-black outside. The nearest public bus stop is a half-hour walk from the campus. He is standing at the stop, warming his hands, when a Saab pulls over.

"Let me give you a ride," says Jude. "You'll freeze to death. North or south?"

Lee looks around, then gets in. "North."

"Good. That's where I'm heading."

They ride in silence past Osborne Village.

"What are you in for?" she says.

"I'm not in for anything."

"You must be. Did you get into some trouble at your old school?"

"It's nothing like that at all." The reason he is at the school, the mathematics, suddenly seems like an intimate secret. "What are you in for?"

"My father went to this school. I'm the only child, the son he never had."

Suddenly his secrets don't seem too heavy. "I'm here for the math program," he says.

"That's beautiful. Good for you."

Lee tells her to head east towards Main Street instead of west. When they pass Portage and Main, he tells her to turn left on Bannatyne Avenue, to the Exchange District, with its turn-of-the-century brick-and-stone office buildings aspiring to the grandeur of Chicago's skyline. He tells her that this is his stop.

"You live here?" she says.

"Somewhere around here. I'm meeting some people."

As soon as she drops him off, he is standing at another bus stop.

...

It is dark when he gets home. There is an empty taxicab parked out front. To his surprise, his mother is inside. He did not know that she has the night off, and has company.

She and a man with a moustache are sitting cross-legged on the living room hardwood floor, a picnic blanket of newspapers on which are plates of *banh xeo* — Vietnamese crepes — whole prawns, and half-empty bowls of fish sauce. They are done eating. Lee can tell that they have been smoking as well because there is a single candle in the middle of the newspaper spread, the flame to clear the air of smoke.

"Why so late?" asks his mother.

"Homework."

The man she is with is named Bao. A social worker, his mother says, although he drives a cab on the side. Going out with a Namer is a change in style for her. She went out with white guys when they first moved here. Some with money. Some who didn't know her real age, that she was older than she said she was. It's because of the pigtails and pink lipstick his mother sometimes wears. They had no idea how old she was until they met Lee. Then they hightailed it.

"You work at a restaurant too?" asks Bao.

"It's his school uniform," says his mother.

"He goes to one of those?"

"He has a gift for mathematics. He got a scholarship."

"It's called a bursary," says Lee.

"Sure, I've heard of those," says Bao. "I also heard you were good at math." Although they have never met, Bao knows enough about Lee to make him squeamish. And it's knowledge that doesn't come from his mother, even; rather, it's just how the community is. Bao knows the business of every boy whom Lee has grown up with, the ones in jail, the ones still dealing freely, the cars they drive, the girls they are seeing. Their families all go to the same church.

As Bao gets up to leave, he grabs Lee's shoulder in a fatherly way, the shoulder that stings. Lee winces. He hands Lee his card, with the address of the immigrants' community centre where Bao is a volunteer.

"Call me any time," Bao says, before leaving to start his shift in his cab.

...

Jude is like a figure on a Roman urn, some mix between lady and beast. She stands at five foot eleven, just on the edge of freakish. Her blonde hair, short in the back and perfectly tousled in the front, is in the windblown style of Amelia Earhart. Her bright, broad, open face is soft in every manner except for two stubbornly hard places: her eyes and chin. She is big in the bone, svelte around the hips, light in her step, heavy in the bosom. She has an intelligence both diamond sharp and coarse, filtered through a husky prairie drawl. She is both elegant and unwieldy, a beast made of gold. To Lee, Jude's elegance radiates through her fingertips, where she spins out her magical computer code.

...

They find each other on the riverbank, both smoking. He thinks he is the only one there.

Jude is leaning against a birch tree, the one with its branches hanging over the swollen river. She holds a cigarette in a fingerless black glove, teardrops slipping off her stone-cold eyes, the way the leaves fall off the birch to be stolen away by the current. Resolution has been all but worn from her face, except for her stubborn chin.

"You'll drown your cigarette at the rate you're going," says Lee.

She wipes her face with her free hand, perhaps to humour him. He thinks he knows why she's crying, so there's no reason to talk about it.

"You know, this tree, it reminds me of the painting in the computer class," says Lee. "Branches hanging over the water. Kind of serene." It seems like the right thing to say, and Lee only realizes that it is a silly comment after he says it. Jude, for the first time, looks right at Lee and her eyes soften. Perhaps she is humouring him again.

"The painting isn't meant to be serene. There are blossoms falling, not leaves, which means premature death, or something."

Lee can see the painting in his mind. "That's too deep. You're making it up."

"Well, the artist has been dead for a thousand years, so we'll never know, will we?"

"So how do you know?"

"My dad bought that painting." Lee returns Jude's hard look. "He donated it to the school."

"So you're Jude Dunster. The Dunster Computer Room."

"Pleased to make your acquaintance." Jude finishes her cigarette and flicks the butt into the river. "Do you have another?" she says.

He shares his last Player's with her. When they leave the river, he smells of cigarettes and lipstick. They dodge other people to make it back to the computer room, where the rest of her cigarettes are in her bag. They continue their smoking after class. It is already dark, and on the way to the riverbank Jude stops under the lighted porte cochère and takes out a small white bottle.

"Eye drops," she says, and tips her head back. It is so cold that he can see the steam rising from her eyes.

They quickly finish the other pack, but they are not ready to stop smoking. They make a 7-Eleven run in her car. He stands in front of the Sev, opening his fresh pack of Player's while watching a couple of skateboarders, but she won't let him take out a cigarette.

"Let's go somewhere more interesting," she says. She drives to Grosvenor Avenue, and they walk to a grocery store that looks closed. The door is unlocked. Inside, it is so dark that he bumps into a Popsicle freezer. "Watch your step," says Jude, who is in front of him. She turns around to tug his sleeve, urge him forward.

It takes a moment for his eyes to adjust to the darkness, and at first all he sees are fireflies scattered throughout the black void of an otherwise empty store. Then his eyes begin to distinguish moving shadows, and he realizes that he is in a room full of other people. In the centre of the store, in front of the cash register, where there should be rows of dry goods, there are instead tables with diners.

"We can smoke in here," she says. Cigarettes, in fact, provide the main illumination in the room. A smattering of the tables have a tea-light candle, but Jude waves off the offer from the waitress.

"Let's just sit in the dark," she says. "We don't do that enough." There is a catch in Lee's throat and she adds: "I meant as a society."

Lee can see hints of the red Coca-Cola button sign on the wall behind the cash register. He can make out Jude's face only when she brings the cigarette close to her to drag, and even then her features are only illuminated in splotches, a spotlight on one eye, part of her cheekbone, the edge of her lip, intensifying Lee's focus on these parts of her. The only time he can make out her whole face is during the billow of light that strikes her when she flicks her Bic for another cigarette.

In the dark she is more of an abstraction, more a ghostly presence, an oracle of code. He wants to sit back and let her explain to him the intricacies of her routines and subroutines. Yet he understands that miracles are ultimately inexplicable. He would settle for listening to her read her code straight-up, watch her little mouth inhale smoke and exhale C++.

She is desolate. "I miss my friends," she says. "But my father went to this school, and so did my grandfather. He slapped his face when he found out it was going coed, like he was trying to wake himself up from a dream, he was so happy. He thought he would have to skip a generation. But here I am."

"So you listen to your dad. You're a good girl."

"I'm really not," she says. Her eyes are so hard at this moment, he can see them glitter in the darkness. "Good at listening, that is."

"Girls can't have real friendships, anyway," says Lee.

"What?"

"It's all based on talk. Real friends suffer in silence with each other."

"Right, I see where you're going. You've got to go to war to make real friends. Well, if only you knew."

"If you hate it here so much, why don't you just leave?"

"It's a good education, if you can survive the people."

He wants to talk about computers. Jude wants to talk about *The Tale of Kieu.*

"Whose tail?" he says.

"It's a Vietnamese folk tale. Part of your national story. How can you not know it?" All he can see of Jude is a sliver of her jawline where it is illuminated by her cigarette.

He cannot tell if she is serious because he cannot see her expression. He does not answer, going through his memory bank for any reference to *The Tale of Kieu* from his mother.

"I've never heard of it," says Lee.

"I'm sorry, I didn't mean to be condescending," says Jude. "It's about a prostitute. But not really, because she was forced into it by her husband. I read a French translation that my father brought home from one of his travels. It's funny that the greatest Vietnamese epic poem is a hooker's survival tale." When Lee doesn't respond, Jude says, "I mean that as a good thing."

When they are done their last pack, Lee has her drop him off at the Exchange District again. If this is an odd thing to do, Jude does not make him feel as if he has to explain himself.

When Lee gets home, he finds Bao with his mother. They are sitting at the table, two glasses and a bottle of beer between them.

"It's bitter," she says.

"It's the hops," says Bao. "It's not that bitter. It's more spicy."

His mother's face is flushed. He has never seen her drink before. Around her wrist is a jade bracelet that Lee cannot place.

"Have a taste," says Bao.

"I'm okay," says Lee.

"Try some," says his mother. "So you can follow what we are talking about."

To get to his own room, he has to walk past a narrow space between the dining table and the couch. Lee has to turn sideways to get through, and has to brush by the couple at the table.

"Say good night to Anh Bao," says his mother.

"Good night," says Lee, without looking at either of them.

...

Lee finds Jude alone on a bitterly cold day in the middle of January, when the river has frozen over and the leaning birch tree looks so brittle in the sunlight, as if it could shatter from within. They are smoking from their own packs of cigarettes. This big-boned girl in her fingerless gloves seems unperturbed. Lee's bare fingers feel as if they are on fire.

She gives him a look of pity, throws the rest of her cigarette onto the icy river, removes both her gloves, and stuffs them into her jacket pocket. Then she blows smoke into her hands, places his hands in hers, and warms them. Her hands dwarf his. He leans into her—leans up to her—and they kiss, her head slightly lowered, his heels slightly raised above the balls of his feet. At first there is a brush of the lips like a lift in the breeze, and then a fluttering of greater urgency.

He unwraps her scarf, and reaches underneath her sweater. Jude reclaims Lee's hands in hers.

"It's cold," she says. A piece of him dies. "Let's get inside."

They do not go back to class, as he had expected, but instead she leads him to the old mansion and down a set of steps, to the boarding girls' laundry room. The sound of the boiler obliterates the noise outside, and they are in a world of fresh sheets that they have spread against cold concrete.

One of his hands is enveloped in hers as they lie down. He removes her sweater with his other hand. Each of her breasts is the size of his face. The flickering moment when his first girl becomes real, not merely as an idea but flesh to his touch, is a revelation. But it is a pleasure that dies all too quickly, as flesh, made real, suddenly becomes a mountain to climb, and Lee realizes that he is not fully equipped. His mind is consumed by a single thought: they don't have a condom.

He gets off Jude with the heaviness of a man getting out of the deep end of a pool. He puts his shirt back on.

"What gives?" she says.

He does not want to say what is topmost on his mind, and so he digs a little deeper into the sediment of consciousness. And this is what he pulls out of the mud: "You should meet my mother."

A lifetime's worth of expressions pass through Jude's face before she finally says, "That would be nice."

...

It is Sunday morning and Lee wakes up to the sight of Bao at the breakfast table, fiddling with something electronic.

Since he has entered their lives, Bao has fixed the leaky faucet in the kitchen, installed a new television, and changed the tiles in the bathroom. He's mowed the lawn in the backyard, even though it's the landlord's property and, strictly speaking, none of their business.

His mother is still asleep in her room. As Lee passes Bao along the narrow space between the table and the couch, he brushes against the table and disturbs whatever it is that Bao is working on. Lee tips his cap and walks right past him.

"You're not going to have something to eat?" says Bao. "I'll make you *banh xeo*."

"Thanks," says Lee. "But I'm okay." He walks out into the backyard, where the cold stings his face. He gets into the 1984 Passat, which has the body of a station wagon, a hatchback ass, and the colour of piss-smudged snow.

The car, however, will not start, even though it has been plugged in. He turns the key again, but there is nothing, nothing, and then a wild buckling from the steering wheel that sends tremors down his arms to his shoulders. He kills the engine. His teeth hurt from chattering.

Bao has followed him outside and is standing by the car. "That was loud," he says. Lee has no idea what the problem is. "Pop open the hood," says Bao.

While Lee sits inside, Bao is standing outside in the cold, under the hood. Lee doesn't want to seem so helpless and needy, and so he gets out. The engine looks like a puzzle that Lee does not have the energy to solve.

"Probably a bum cylinder," says Bao. "Just have to figure out which one. Turn the engine back on." Lee hesitates a moment, for no other reason than because Bao is telling him to do something. Then he relents and sends the car back into convulsions. Meanwhile, Bao has gone to his cab to pull out a tool kit. Then, with the softest hands Lee has ever seen on a man, Bao disconnects each of the spark plug wires, one at a time. As he disconnects each wire, the buckling dies a little.

"Got it," says Bao. "Notice when I cut this wire, but nothing happened to the engine? This must be the one." Bao pulls out a spark plug, presses it to Lee's face. "Can you see that?" says Bao. "It's cracked. I'll go to the Canadian Tire to get another one. Can you wait?"

"Take your time," says Lee. "I've got all day."

"I'm taking your mother to church today," says Bao. "You should come. Meet some good kids in the neighbourhood."

"It's okay," says Lee. "I'm really a Buddhist."

"Oh yeah. How'd you get that way?"

Lee just shrugs his shoulders. "Caught it from someone passing through."

Bao smiles at Lee through his moustache. "I'll see you later."

...

Lee doesn't see Jude for most of the week. She isn't avoiding him so much as avoiding the whole school. She isn't in computer class, and if not there, she won't be in any class. He starts to hallucinate her, thinks he catches glimpses of her down hallways, hears echoes of mooing down the corners of the hallways where the jocks lumber by, but he isn't sure.

On Friday she is back in computer class, the last class of the day. He sits behind her.

She doesn't turn around the whole time, not even when class is over and the rest of the students file out. She is in her own world, typing code. When she is done, and turns around, she gasps to see him there. "I guess I was focused," she says.

"Have dinner with me," says Lee. "It's late."

"I don't think it's a good idea," she says. "It's frozen outside. I'm calling a cab. I didn't bring my car."

"I brought my car," says Lee. He believes that if he looks at her hard enough, he can will her to come with him. He draws close to her, a move that feels like the bravest thing he has ever done. "I'll keep your hands warm," he says.

Ever since Bao replaced the spark plug, the Passat has been driving like a charm. Lee thinks Jude expected him to take her to Osborne Village, because when he drives past this hip neighbourhood—with its bookstores, coffee houses, ale and toad-in-the-hole pubs—Jude asks him where they are going. "A place in my neighbourhood," says Lee. He takes her to his mother's diner on Ellice Avenue.

His mother has started working nights again. It is just the start of her shift, yet it is already pitch-black outside. Inside, the fluorescent lighting reflects off a newly mopped linoleum floor. The restaurant is almost deserted; they have their pick of the varnished wood tables in the smoking section or the padded vinyl booths in the family section. Lee takes Jude to the counter.

"Is this smoking?" says Jude.

"Non-smoking," says Lee.

"Odd," says Jude, but Lee insists they sit down.

His mother comes out from the kitchen, apron, name tag, hairnet. He is relieved that she is not in pigtails. Her eyes go wide when she sees her son at the counter. Lee has never stopped to visit before. He is a wonder in his mother's eyes.

"Jude, this is my mother," says Lee.

Both women are flustered, but Jude manages to crack a smile for both of them. When the two women touch hands, it is as if they are each reaching across dimensions. His mother hands two plastic menus to Lee, one of which he gives to Jude. There is nowhere to hide in an empty restaurant, and so his mother spends most of the time in the kitchen. His mother avoids direct eye contact, yet he catches her gaze reflected off the metal forks and water glasses that she serves them.

"Her English isn't so good," says Lee.

"That's perfectly all right," says Jude.

She orders, through Lee, the liver, onions, and mashed potatoes. He asks his mother the same for himself, just to keep Jude company. Then he tells Jude that her code is the most elegant thing he has ever seen. He speaks about all of his doubts as a coder. He has such a facility for abstractions, he is a master of the language of mathematics on the page, but he cannot turn this into life on the screen. It is a dimension he cannot break through.

Jude listens to him while he unburdens himself. Lee is so busy talking he has barely touched his food by the time her plate is licked clean. It's okay, he has no appetite at the moment. He tells Jude to switch plates, so that his mother won't hassle him about not eating when she comes to pick them up.

"She'll think I didn't like the food," says Jude.

"She'll think you're being a lady," says Lee.

His mother brings them bowls of vanilla ice cream and fruit cups for dessert. When they get up to leave, she gives them each a cookie, wrapped in a napkin. When he gets Jude into his car, he feels the night is opening up to endless opportunities. He's going to take Jude back to his house. His mother will be at the restaurant for the rest of the night.

"Take me home," says Jude.

"What? It's still early."

"Not for around here."

"What do you mean 'not for around here'?"

"I'm tired. Please."

He does a U-turn around Ellice Avenue. It is then that he notices that the Passat has a new dashboard radio. Bao must have installed it while replacing the spark plug. It's a garish thing, too shiny and new for the rest of the car. He can't get the radio out of his mind when he turns into the long private driveway of Jude's house on Wellington Crescent.

Lee had thought about trying to change her mind, but when he drives up to the elegant brick fortress that is her house, he can only muster a feeble "see you" as Jude hustles out of the car, leaving footprints on the moon-white snow as she disappears from his view.

Lee, driving home, makes a detour onto Maryland Street. He rips out the dashboard radio, tucks it under his arm, and treads with it through the snow, through a small tinted-glass door that conceals the larger space behind it.

This is the immigrants' community centre where Bao volunteers. Next door is the women's shelter where one morning Lee came to pick his mother up. The community centre is a space that Lee has been in before, with the card and mah-jong tables set up for the old men, the ping-pong tables that are cleared at night to make way for bedding, and the large canteen of tea on the sidelines of a gymnasium-like space, like a remnant of a bygone prom. He strides past a cloud of smoke where the card tables are, bumping into elbows, which releases a fluttering of cards and curses, past the overhanging curtain into the sleeping space, knocking his feet against sleeping bodies because his eyes have not adjusted to the darkness.

There is a promise of light on the other side of a curtain. Past the curtain is a little warren of offices and a worn-out couch in the hallway, where he finds Bao smoking and reading a magazine.

Before Bao looks up, Lee has just enough time to rehearse, once again in his head, what he had wanted to tell Bao the first time he saw him.

The Fig Tree off Knight Street

We did not tell our mothers why we suddenly refused their meats. We just left them on our plates — the pork chops, lemon grass chicken, tilapia, whatever they were — and ate the rice and vegetables served underneath. If the meat lay hidden in a stew, then we drank the soup until the clams or scallops or prawn eyes emerged whole to dry out in the air. Of course, we knew we would suffer for this. Some of our mothers spanked us, some sent us early to bed, and some shed tears to make us feel guilty, as if the animals we waved away were being dealt another death blow at our little hands. But we would not capitulate. At the time, we were aping Thanh, the boy who cured Yen. We would not, of course, give him up to our mothers, at least not for a while. Instead, when they pleaded with their greasy hands for an explanation, we said we were just doing ourselves some good. We thought then, as many of us still do now, that of all Thanh's traits we could have aped, his disavowal of the flesh was the least peculiar.

Some of us first met Thanh in ESL class, some outside on the steel climbing dome. Those late joining our group met him at the little parking lot off Knight Street. Thanh was fresh to Vancouver and had spent his life in a Communist Vietnamese re-education camp. He didn't speak a lick of English. And yet he walked our grounds with a weary stoop, as if he was already too familiar with the terrain. He seemed older than us, though he was no taller. He lacked our fidgety energy. His air of quiet resignation was unchanging, whether he sat still in class listening to the teachers speak incomprehensibly above him, or ran at full pace while being chased by larger boys around the concrete track.

We heard that Thanh lived with some distantly related uncle and an ill mother who spoke only to herself and her son. We heard that Thanh's father was some American GI whom Thanh had never met. When he and his mother were let out of the re-education camp, his mother had the option of moving to America but decided on Canada because she couldn't face the possibility, however remote, of encountering this GI again. Any GI, for that matter.

Thanh was almost Vietnamese in every way; there was nothing to betray him as the son of an American except for his faintly violet eyes, as if they had once been a piercing blue but were now daubed with blood. We pitied him, for each of his rubber sandals, neither of which was shaped particularly for the right or left foot; for his uneven, matted bangs that stuck to his forehead; and for a ghastly odour that trailed him, provoking us to offer him our fresh socks or T-shirts. Those who could speak some Vietnamese did our best to translate the lessons for him, though it was hard, because most of us were not born there and were therefore not fluent. When Thanh was absent from school, which seemed more often than not, we tried to devise excuses to mollify his teachers so that they wouldn't search for him at his home.

We pitied him, but we did not take him seriously—that is, until he cured mute Yen. She had stopped talking on her first day of kindergarten and we had all heard how Thanh had, months later, shaken her voice free. How Yen, on the way home from school, was chased by a one-eared dog. How she turned off Knight Street and ran down a rutted alleyway that was bordered by the backyard fencing of Vancouver Specials on one side and little parking spaces behind the pharmacies, grocery stores, and flower shops on the other side. She ran until she reached a dead end just beyond the parking stalls of a German butcher shop, to a wooden fence that was too high to climb over. There was, however, a way through: the fence had a rotted-out gap in the shape of a flame. On the other side was the backyard where a large fig tree grew, its branches cascading over the fence, weighed down by leaves. Though the air had been still just moments before, the branches of the fig tree were rattling. Yen got down on all fours, was about to scoot through the gap in the fence when Thanh emerged through it from the other side. He wielded a broken lamp base. They say that the sight of Thanh and his violet eyes, compounded by the barking dog and the rattling fig tree, made Yen scream.

Of course, we had to see what it was that had startled her. One day after school a small cadre followed Yen on that same path. Some of us wanted to see the fig tree, an unusual creature here in East Vancouver, long ago cleared of its old-growth conifers, which were replaced by stucco homes in neighbourhoods speckled with spindly maple and plum trees. Others of us were simply wondering what Thanh was up to, since he had not shown up to school that day. As soon as we turned off Knight Street and its paved sidewalk to the rutted alleyway, we felt as if we had stepped into the wilderness. We sidestepped rain-filled potholes and walked gingerly through rough, slippery gravel. The wood and chain-link fencing of the homes grew taller the deeper we walked in. And yet we felt more exposed to the elements. While on Knight Street the only breeze was from the hush of traffic, and little puffy clouds hung dormant in the sky. As soon as we turned the bend to our destination we felt a gush of wind that lifted our skirts or our jackets and our hair. The fig tree shook as if we had startled it, and we trembled from a noise that was a tripartite crying of pigs, sheep, and chickens.

We now believe that there was something peculiar in the geography or construction of the alleyway that gathered the breezes into itself. We did not have an explanation then. And we still don't have one for how the horns from the distant traffic or the pounding of the butcher's knife from the nearby store were transformed by the wind into those animal noises. When we got to within ten feet of the wooden fence, which was marked off by the last painted white stripe of a parking stall, we stopped and waited for the air to calm. It eventually did, as we remember it, when Thanh emerged through the flame-shaped gap in the fence. Then those barnyard cries were replaced by a human's, which we knew was Thanh's mother talking to herself through her open kitchen window. We could tell from the fresh oil burns freckling his hand, from an overpowering smell of food in his hair, and from his sweaty brow that he was in the middle of cooking something. The younger among us felt envy at the licence he was given to play with stoves at his age. Those of us who were older felt pity at what this licence meant.

Thanh looked into each of our eyes, until he was sure we were not an angry mob. Then he smiled. "You look scared," he said, to no one in particular. Some of us took that as a challenge to our resolve and clenched our jaws. The youngest among us just nodded.

From his jeans pockets Thanh pulled a large gold amulet with a hole in the middle, wrapped in a piece of cloth. It was almost the diameter of a puck and had on it unusual figures etched in relief. Its light made us shiver, yet helped us see why our mothers loved gold.

Thanh bent down on one knee and placed the cloth on the white stripe of the parking stall, then the amulet on top of the cloth, then stood up again.

"Where did you get that?" asked little Yen. The rest of us pulled her back.

"Stay on your side," he said in Vietnamese, motioning to the amulet and the white stripe, "and you'll have nothing to be scared of."

Meanwhile, Thanh stayed on his side of the white line, under the fig branches by the fence. He sat down on the cracked asphalt and crossed his legs. We all sat down and crossed our legs as well.

We asked him how he cured Yen. Thanh smiled peevishly, brushed the dust off his lap, and shook his head, as if embarrassed by the question. "I cannot say," he said, and was silent after that, content to pick at the ground for oddly coloured pebbles. It was not long until we became fidgety, as if we were back in class.

We told Thanh that since we were all sitting here cross-legged in this parking lot, he might as well tell us our fortunes. "I don't tell fortunes," he said. We didn't believe him and couldn't hold back our disappointment, because just as he said this, his hair became ruffled as if by some invisible hand, though there had not been a breeze for some time.

He blew the hair out of his eyes and sighed, then stood up. He said he had to go home. He was hungry. But if we came back next time with "something useful," then maybe he'd talk. Then he disappeared back through the flame, and we got up to retrace our steps through the alleyway, back to Knight Street.

Of course, the next time that Thanh skipped class, we came looking for him after school. We had to overcome our fears of that alleyway — of the sudden wind and noises — and so we each brought along our own objects of comfort. When we made it to the dead-end fence, we stopped just short of the white parking stripe, just as Thanh had told us. We stood there, enduring the cries of the pigs, sheep, and chickens, until Thanh emerged and all those noises disappeared and all we could hear was Thanh's mother scolding herself in the distance. We waited until Thanh placed the cloth and the amulet upon the white stripe and sat down cross-legged. Then we each took out something from our knapsacks. One of us brought a little figurine of the Virgin Mary that she placed on the white stripe. Another had a rosewood carving of the Buddha, while another had a picture of the Bodhisattva Quan Am and rosaries. Others placed their favourite Star Wars action figure, or a Care Bear, or a rubber parachute man. I had a plastic Battle Cat (of the *He-Man* series), with its bared fangs and yellow stripes set against a green suggestion of fur so smooth that you could pet it along the grain in any direction. I took my figurine out of my knapsack and placed it among the rest of our little protective friends.

We also brought candies. There were boxes of jaw-breakers. There were lime and grape Nerds that were like sparkling, rough-hewn grains of kryptonite. There were also Runts—these iridescently lacquered, tiny fruit dolls—and solid bars of Mackintosh's toffee. We piled all of these into an offering for Thanh. At this Thanh smiled, opened a box of Runts, and told us to share the rest of the candies among ourselves. Now, as he chewed on hard candies, he was in the mood to talk. We sat there and gorged on sugar while Thanh spoke to us idly of the confections of our ancestors: of sweetened rice wafers and tamarinds that you ate and kept the seeds to play marbles with, of candied nuts and agar-agar jelly. All of this talk made the Nerds, Runts, and jawbreakers seem insubstantial. Their sugars melted in our mouths and left nothing but stains on our tongues. It was then that Thanh spoke of the perils of eating meat. Our faces turned red as we listened, and some of us put our hands on our stomachs.

Thanh's lesson on meat ended just when we finished all the candies. He was quiet again, picking at the ground for shiny pebbles. We were both agitated and emboldened by our sugar rush and could not endure the silence for very long. We demanded that Thanh tell us our fortunes.

Once again, Thanh told us that he was no fortune teller. He said, however, that he knew something of our pasts, which was for us something more elusive. He knew how our ancestors died. Some of us didn't believe him. "Well, then, who wants to go first?" he said. We all looked at each other and no one raised their hand.

Thanh looked at each of us, then uncrossed his legs

and stood up. "You aren't at all curious?" he said. When we still didn't answer, he turned his back to us as if he was going to leave. We clapped our hands so that he would stay. We told him that we would hear a story. He sat down and crossed his legs again. All he needed from us was a little piece of information, our names or our parents' names. Maybe the city or village where they came from. He squinted at us, as if trying to see the resemblance between us and the faces he conjured in his mind. He finished his first story about one little girl's grandmother whom she'd never met, and then waited to let the little girl wipe away her tears before moving on to the next story. Despite the tears, none of us were ready to leave, and so he started on another story, then another. Those who understood Vietnamese translated for those who did not.

We heard of someone who was shot by friendly fire from the Hac Bao army company, then of someone who fell off a cliff in the wet jungle while carrying artillery because he wore rubber sandals without traction. One of us had the blood of a poet in his veins who died in prison starving himself, because the Communists had confiscated his sheaf of love poems, unsure if they were harmless odes to his wife or to counter-revolutionary ideals. We nodded with understanding; sometimes our parents took our poems or drawings or comics away.

When it got dark, we knew we would be scolded at home. We gathered our belongings and made our way back to Knight Street. Afterwards, we tried to verify these stories with our parents, but surreptitiously, without giving Thanh away as the source. Mostly our parents dismissed them in some vague way that only made us more suspicious. They weren't interested in hearing all this old news and told us to exercise some discipline over our imaginations. And they were too busy working double shifts, making us dinner, or scratching lottery tickets to replace these stories with their own.

We never raised these subjects with Thanh when we saw him under normal circumstances. Instead, we lent him our bikes or gave him our extra T-shirts (he was particularly fond of the Whitecaps), or helped ward off the bullies who stalked him for his eyes. We gave him a pair of KangaROOS shoes with Velcro straps and little pockets on the tongues so he wouldn't have to fuss with laces and would have something to keep his pebbles in. We admired him for qualities that would have brought each of us into disrepute: how he had never watched TV and never combed his hair; how he could scamper barefoot up even the skinniest of East Vancouver's plum trees; how he never rode a bike until we taught him and, when we did, how quickly he learned. He loved our bikes, and we were envious that he had no one to scold him about zigzagging from sidewalk to road and back, or to warn him not to rush through stop signs with his ankles raised on the handlebars instead of down on the pedal brakes.

But it was just a matter of time before we betrayed him. It took only one weak link, one child like Yen to be given a good spanking for refusing her mother's meat, for Thanh's name to be mentioned. And it wasn't long before one or two of us revealed to our parents the ritual in the butcher's parking lot. Our parents, in return, clucked their tongues against the roofs of their mouths knowingly. They knew of Thanh and his mother and told us that they never lived together in the same re-education camp, but rather the Communists would have separated them when Thanh was an infant for "moral reasons," which explained why Thanh was so unkempt and why his mother talked herself into a craziness. It was only recently that the two had been reunited. Our parents told us that his stories most likely came from his mother during her endless soliloquies. We shouldn't take them so seriously.

But still we went back to the parking lot and sat down with Thanh the next opportunity we had. We wanted to hear more, no matter what our parents said. Yet what we were interested in was not so much the causes of our ancestors' deaths. We had heard too many stories of them having not enough food or swallowing too much salt water or of thatched roofs glowing with fire in the night. So many that Thanh's voice was bland and his eyes went dull when he told them. What we wanted to hear instead was what Thanh could not tell us, what our unknowable loved ones were holding in their hands in their last moments—a gun, a pen, beads, another loved one's hand. Still, we listened to Thanh, and huddled together against the chilly air while looking down at our own empty hands.

More than anything, we wanted to come as close as we could to the source of these stories, and we knew that we could not stop with Thanh. And so, on what turned out to be our last day with him, we left school early. Instead of going back to class after recess, we gathered our knapsacks and headed down Knight Street. When we reached the mouth of the alleyway, the older ones zippered the jackets of the younger ones before we turned into it and faced the whipping winds. We covered our ears when we heard the pigs, sheep, and chickens. We knew that Thanh would be at home, but when we reached that last white stripe, we did not sit down and we did not wait for him. Instead, we walked across the stripe and entered his backyard through the flame-shaped gap. Those of us who were small enough walked through, while the rest of us got down on our hands and knees.

The grass grew wild in his backyard and was covered with a dusting of dandelion fluff. We stepped on dead figs, which gave way softly beneath our feet like curled-up mice. We walked towards the sound of the barn animals, which seemed to come from a window on the second floor of the house. When we reached the wooden stairs to the balcony, with its flaking blue paint, these animal cries yielded to a single insistent voice. It was Thanh's mother, whom we were looking for on that day.

The first one of us to reach the top of the balcony knocked on the door. We waited in a descending line, holding on to the creaking banister, which shook from both the breezes and our weight, holding on to each other's hands like slipping climbers, until Thanh's mother opened the door and let us in. She didn't look surprised to see us, only sad. One by one we filed into her little dining room. She pulled her jet-black hair back into a bun, which had the effect of smoothing out some of the wrinkles on her forehead. She wore a bright yellow *ao dai* with a floral pattern, dressed for some special Vietnamese occasion that our parents were too busy to tell us about. Her face looked tired, but no more tired than our parents' faces. Her body was svelte and wrapped tightly beneath the *ao dai*, and she walked around the dining table with a vigour that belied the look in her eyes when they met ours. She was talking the whole time, not to any one of us, but to herself or to some imaginary person standing next to her. She never stopped talking to herself even when she stared at us and motioned for us to take our jackets off and directed us to our seats. Then she disappeared into the kitchen, her voice trailing over her shoulder.

At first we didn't smell food, only incense. We saw against the wall an altar with a photo of an ancient couple who could have been the grandparents of any one of us, saw the smoking joss sticks whose ash tips lengthened, greyed, and curled like the fingernails of this same couple. It was then that Thanh appeared, and for the first time we were truly scared. His hair was tangled as if he had been standing in a windstorm. He was wearing one of our Whitecaps shirts and clutching his lamp base, which he raised over his head. We realized that he had been sleeping the whole day. He looked at us with both anger and fear.

Then his mother came back into the dining room and in a moment of lucidity looked Thanh in the eyes and spoke to him directly. "Let them be," she said. Then she turned back to the kitchen and Thanh started to follow her. "Sit with them," she said. "I don't need your help." We heard the kitchen windows close.

Thanh put down the lamp base and sat down on a fold-out chair, more than ever like one of us. We knew they rented this house with some sort of uncle, but didn't dare ask where this uncle was. Meanwhile, we could hear his mother humming in the kitchen over the spatter of oil. Restless Yen got off her seat and took a peek inside the kitchen, then scampered back to us trying to hold back her giggling. She had seen Thanh's mother bent over a red bucket filled with soap water and set on the ground, washing her hands in the bucket instead of the sink.

We tried to sit politely until Thanh's mother came out and set the table, leaning over us as if we weren't there. Afterwards, she brought out the food—no meat, of course. The smell of it made us crazy with hunger. She brought out steaming pots, sizzling and popping bowls, and dishes cold as a corpse. We ate as if our parents had never fed us in our lives.

She sat down with us, but she didn't touch her handiwork. Mostly she talked softly but rapidly, as if in a chant. Every so often she would interrupt her own rhythm with a shriek and other sharp-sounding utterances, making us jump up from our seats. Both apologies and accusations spewed from her, her voice as animated as her face was expressionless. We weren't sure if she was talking to one imaginary person or if she herself was taking on several roles. At times it sounded as though she was yelling at Thanh's father, at other times pleading with a jailer. Once she said, "If you are the Seven Dwarfs, then what am I?" One of us answered, "Snow White!" while little Yen said, "The evil queen!" We shushed them both, told them to let Thanh's mother be. She wasn't talking to us.

Thanh did his best to ignore her, but we knew he wanted us out. She kept her eyes focused on something on the oak-finished tabletop, as if concentrating on its grain at an atomic level. And yet she always noticed from the corner of her eyes when one of us had spooned our last bit of rice and made sure to fill our bowls herself. We had no words to describe her condition at the time, and could only say that she was half in this world, half in another.

When Yen had finished her bowl, she caught Thanh's mother's eye and said: "How did your husband die?" which provoked the little boy next to her to say: "Shut up, Yen, who says he's dead?"

For a moment Thanh's mother closed her mouth and stared at the children, then looked at each of us with such a clear gaze that we could see her sane, beautiful self flickering like a ghost somewhere behind her eyes. Now we wanted to ask what this woman's last moment was like before she became the one standing before us, but instead we held our breaths and let the temptation flicker past. Thanh's face reddened, and we were not sure if it was from anger, embarrassment, or an awful insight into the danger he had created by attracting us here. For the first time we considered our own time on this earth.

Then Thanh's mother resumed talking to herself and everything seemed normal again. We all looked down at our bowls and gorged ourselves until we were stuffed. How could we eat anything our parents gave us now? Of course, our parents asked this too, because when all the food was gone, we could hear the sound of rubber on gravel through the shut windows. We heard our parents in the butcher's parking lot. We heard their approaching footsteps. We got up and grabbed our knapsacks, pulled out our objects of devotion, what our parents so lovingly gave us, and we lined them up on the threshold of the doorway. If not to stop them, then at least to make them pause.

Turkey Day

I hadn't planned on speaking to anyone that day. All I wanted to do, all I had promised to do, was find a turkey.

I was being put up at the Swissôtel by the law firm that employed me. Until less than a month ago my apartment building had stood in the shadows of the World Trade Center. The apartment was still there, but now nothing stood between it and the sunrise. I wasn't allowed to move back in yet. The building was being tested for structural stability and barricaded by the National Guard. Downtown Manhattan still resembled a war zone. The Swissôtel was located a world away, in shiny Midtown.

It was early in the morning. I was, in fact, still in my boxer shorts when I got the call from the lobby. "Mr. Chau," said the concierge. "Your wife is here to see you."

"I don't have a wife," I said. In fact, at the moment, I wasn't sure if I had a girlfriend.

"Just a second," said the concierge. I was put on hold, and listened to static broken by muffled voices in the background.

"Hello?" I said.

"She swears by it," said the concierge. "Can I let her up?"

Before I could reply, the concierge hung up the phone. I hardly had time to put on a shirt and a pair of pants, and to look out the window to catch a glimpse of my favourite tree on Park Avenue before the doorbell rang.

I carried a faint hope that it was Haejin, playing some joke on me, telling me that her answer was, finally, yes. But it was Nga, dressed in a rain jacket, though it was sunny outside. I barely knew her, and only as a client. And yet I knew I should not have been surprised.

"You can't go around lying like that," I said. "You have no reason to say you're my wife."

"I needed to tell them something," she said. Nga had probably never been inside the lobby of such a nice hotel, and felt she needed to give a reason to be here.

My hotel room was well-appointed but small. To get to the living area/study, you had to brush by the bed. It had one chair, which I offered to Nga. I also offered her a cup of coffee, but she waved me away. I took her rain jacket and threw it on my unmade bed.

"The deadline for my filing is today, no?" said Nga, smiling prettily. Her tanned skin made her tea-stained teeth seem lighter. "I have to sign my affidavit?"

"No, it's not due today," I said. "I'm still drafting it." I had her file on my small desk, her "battered spouse" application for permanent residency, as it is known in INS parlance. Nga was from Ben Tre, a little town to the south of Ho Chi Minh City (or Saigon, as she insisted I refer to it). Her husband lived in New Jersey. A couple of years earlier they had met over the phone, long-distance, through a professional matchmaker. They got married last year, and she had left Vietnam for New Jersey. But even before the ink of Nga's green card application was dry, he started "abusing" her. Her word. She needed to leave him, but was scared of losing her conditional permanent residency status and being deported. The immigration laws provided recourse. An alien could still maintain permanent residency status in the United States if she could show that she had entered into a genuine marriage and had to leave the marriage because she was battered by her husband.

"We can finish it today, no?" said Nga. She went to my small desk, picked up a manila envelope with her name on it, and handed it to me.

"I suppose so," I said, "since you're already here." My plans for finding a turkey would have to wait until the afternoon. At least working on the file would distract me from thinking about Haejin. At noon she would be having lunch with her parents, who were visiting from Vancouver. I knew where Haejin would be taking them, even though she had never told me.

Nga's case was in fact the only file I had been working on for the last month. I took it on pro bono, because I was sick of the mundane tasks of junior lawyering for a corporate law firm, my regular fare of reviewing documents for privilege and drafting letters for the partners' signatures. I wanted my own case, and I was referred to Nga because I spoke some Vietnamese, albeit with a heavy Canadian accent. I had been in New York for a year now, and the work I was doing for the law firm seemed so insignificant in the grand scheme of things.

I had already drafted most of the affidavit. I had written Nga's story down as she told me it, from the moment she was introduced to her husband — or at least the idea of him — through a matchmaker. Inside the manila envelope were all the constituent parts of her application: phone records showing all the calls between Trenton and Saigon, where Nga was living; photographs of her husband's first and only visit to Ben Tre to meet Nga and her family; photographs of their two wedding ceremonies, one in a hotel in Saigon, one in Trenton's City Hall. These I would attach as exhibits to the affidavit, her narrative of her voyage from Vietnam to the United States, and the two months of bliss once she arrived here.

"I need one more thing," I said. I was surprised that I couldn't finish the sentence. I was trained in business litigation. I was used to analyzing financial statements and initial public offering prospectuses, not the forma-tion and breakdown of a marriage. What I needed from Nga was intimate.

"What is it?"

"I need to know how your marriage failed."

"It failed because he no longer respects me."

"I understand that," I said. "But does he hit you?" She shook her head. "Does he abuse you in any other way?"

She lifted her eyebrows.

"We need some sort of evidence to make this work," I said. I took out a copy of the Power and Control Wheel that came with my pro bono attorney's packet, which diagrammed all the possible forms of domestic violence, organized inside evenly measured pie slices. We went through them one by one: Using Coercion & Threats; Using Intimidation; Using Emotional Abuse; Using Isolation; Minimizing, Denying, Blaming; Using Children; Using Male Privilege; Using Economic Abuse.

She shook her head as I pointed to each pie slice.

"He's done none of these things?"

"Maybe that one," she said, pointing at Using Emotional Abuse. "And that one," pointing at Using Isolation.

"You'll have to provide details," I said. "Does he bully you?"

"He tries," she said. For the next half-hour she described to me the litany of arguments she had with her husband, over money, over his smoking, over her mother-in-law, how he would abruptly leave in the middle of a yelling match and be gone for days and come home with no explanation.

"And how has this affected you?" I asked, trying to be clinical.

"I have brain damage."

"Brain damage?" I said. It took me a moment. "You mean psychological damage?"

"I can no longer paint. I've lost my concentration. Because of the abuse."

"I didn't know you were a painter," I said. "I thought you did nails."

"*Now*, I do nails," she said. "In Saigon, I painted with lacquer. I was famous."

I suddenly felt tired, though it was only morning. If Nga was telling the truth that she was a professional painter, then I would need to attach reproductions of her paintings to the affidavit, maybe even get reference letters from gallery owners, curators, or customers, and would likely need them to be translated.

"I'll need more evidence," I said. "We're definitely not going to finalize this today. Maybe you can gather the additional materials and we'll reconvene another time." I picked up her rain jacket from the bed and handed it to her. I wanted to be alone, and I needed to get a turkey.

"Okay, then. Let's go."

"Go where?"

"To get the evidence."

"Why do you need me to come with you?"

"Because I can't bring the evidence to you," she said. "You need to see it yourself."

I didn't understand her, and I wasn't sure if it was because my Vietnamese wasn't sufficiently fluent or because she was being deliberately enigmatic. In any event, I knew that Nga would not leave my hotel room without me.

...

On the way to the subway station, I popped my head into a grocery store, but the only turkeys they sold were sliced like ham. Nga could sense my distraction and pulled me back outside by the arm. We took the number 6 train south, towards Lower Manhattan.

"Vancouver is such a beautiful city," said Nga. "I miss Burns Bog very much." I had mentioned to Nga when we first met that I was from Vancouver, and she wouldn't let me forget this fact. Nga told me that on her way from Vietnam to New Jersey, she had arranged to stay with a friend in Vancouver for a few days.

"I can't believe you know anything about Burns Bog," I said.

"Why wouldn't you believe me?"

"Visitors aren't allowed in the area, for one thing. It's a protected ecosystem. Besides, it's not even in Vancouver, it's all the way out in Delta." I had been to Burns Bog once in high school, sneaking past the No Trespass signs with a friend. I don't remember very much about it, other than that the flat landscape with its reeds, ponds, and cranes was very different from the mountains and evergreen forests that surrounded most of Vancouver. I remember walking on what seemed like a carpet of moss. The ground was dry, but the moss undulated and rippled with every step I took, as if I were walking on a waterbed.

"My friend lives in Delta," said Nga. "I told her I wanted to visit a park, and that's where she took me. I miss Vancouver very much."

"Delta is not Vancouver," I said, sounding unconvincing even to myself.

When the Towers fell, all of Lower Manhattan was barricaded, at first all the way up to Union Square. Gradually the barricades moved south as the streets were opened again, down to Canal, then to Houston Street, then beyond. Although trains ran all the way down south to Bowling Green, I still felt uneasy heading in that direction. My pulse quickened when we hit Union Square. I had not been this far south since that day. Luckily, Nga motioned to get out at the next stop, Astor Place. We walked up back into daylight and towards the cavern of Broadway. Almost a month after the event, the air down here was still dustier than in Midtown. The sunlight, when mixed with the dust, grew a darker shade of orange.

"This way," said Nga, touching my elbow. "Across the street." She took me to a set of stairs that drifted down from the sidewalk to a basement door. She rang the doorbell. An old lady opened it and smiled with polished black teeth when she saw Nga. The old lady was Vietnamese as well.

Inside was an art gallery. "They sell only Vietnamese works here," said Nga. "By appointment only."

I had never been to Vietnam, or a place like this. I had expected to feel claustrophobic in a room with low ceilings, but the basement was combined with the ground-level floor to form one loft space, magnifying its airiness. On the walls were paintings of mothers in silk dresses, or of the countryside, or of the imperial palaces of Hue, or the merchant shops of Hoi An. There were pastels, and watercolours, and oils. There was nothing about war, not a hint.

"This is me," said Nga. She took me by the elbow to a display in the corner.

"What are they made of?"

"Lacquer, of course. Can't you tell?"

I had seen lacquer paintings before, in Vietnamese restaurants — those glittering seashell landscapes of temples and buffalo-drawn carts set against a background of polished black. Lacquer paintings reduced life to so many stars twinkling in the night.

But these were different. One was as bright as any pastel. Another was a rendering of the coconut trees of Ben Tre, in as much fine detail as an oil painting. Yet another was a willowy abstract figure painting that could have been mistaken for a watercolour.

"You painted all of these?"

"I did them all in Saigon. I was surprised to find them for sale here, to tell you the truth. They arrived in New York before I did."

"You can find absolutely anything in New York," I said. I would have to come back to take photos of these paintings for Nga's affidavit. "And you say you no longer paint?"

"That's right," said Nga. "Because of the abuse."

How could I make this evidence convincing? I would need details of how many times she had tried but failed to paint in New Jersey, and how it was all connected to whatever her husband did to her.

Then I noticed the clock on a wall, a bright-blue installation that I thought was one of the paintings. It was half past eleven. Haejin would soon be having lunch with her parents. My chest seized. I needed fresh air.

"You'll have to excuse me," I said.

I stepped out into the sunlight. A young mother with a stroller brushed by. She smiled. How we'd all changed since that day. Strangers made eye contact on the street, on the subway, and smiled. Happy to be alive. It was almost a month later, and still.

I felt a hand on my shoulder. "Where are you going?" It was Nga. She had a look of utter concern on her face, for me.

"You know what?" I said. "We are having lunch." Nga nodded her head matter-of-factly.

We walked back up to Union Square. I ducked into a bodega, but again no turkey. We took the N train from Union Square to 32nd Street. We were in Little Korea. I took Nga up a flight of rickety iron stairs to Haejin's favourite restaurant.

It was a tight space, with little round tables and a small bar at the front. I took a seat against a window, facing the entrance, while Nga faced me. I did not see Haejin. After a while, sipping water, Nga asked me, "Where are the menus?"

"There are no menus here," I said. "They sell only one thing. Double-fried chicken wings."

"Okay, then," said Nga. "But I have to warn you, I am not hungry."

"You don't like fried chicken?"

"I do. I am just not in the mood for it."

"Trust me," I said. "You will be when it comes." I felt no conviction for the words that I mouthed. I was not in the mood for double-fried chicken either.

Haejin arrived before our order did. She came in through the entrance ahead of her mother and father, and stared at me from the threshold, the whites of her eyes widening like spilt milk just as on that morning the previous month. I could tell from her expression that it took all of her willpower not to turn around, to proceed normally. They were seated across from us, in my plain view.

Her parents looked kindly, both in baseball caps, a little frumpy from cross-country travel, not the stern ogres that Haejin had made them out to be. They owned a flower store in East Vancouver. I grew up in the same neighbourhood, though my path never crossed Haejin's, not until I was at UBC studying law and Haejin was studying fine art at Emily Carr.

Our chicken arrived.

"You were right," said Nga. "I didn't know how hungry I was." She dug into the chicken wings.

I could tell that Haejin was straining to ignore me while talking to her parents, while I was distracted by the crackling of Nga's incisors through crispy skin and into bone.

"You're not eating," said Nga. "Still hungry?"

"Not really," I said. "My fiancée is sitting behind you, with her parents. Well, almost fiancée. Don't turn around."

"What do you mean 'almost fiancée'?"

"I proposed to her last week."

"She rejected you?"

"Not quite," I said. "She said she would think about it."

"What type of ring did you get for her?"

"I didn't have a ring."

"How could you propose without a ring?"

"I don't know," I said. "It was spur-of-the-moment."

"So why are you not over there?" Nga gave a little nod of her head when she said that, to indicate the table behind her.

"I wanted to meet her parents, but Haejin refused. So here I am. With you."

Nga nodded. I grabbed a chicken wing and we ate in silence. I paid the cheque when it came.

Nga and I were the first to leave. When I walked by Haejin's table, she tightened her lips in abject scorn. Outside, I said goodbye to Nga at the entrance of the N line.

"When will I see you again?" she said.

"As soon as you get more evidence," I said. Tears appeared in her eyes. All I could do was put my hand on her cheek and brush away a tear with my finger.

"My marriage was real."

"I know that."

She disappeared down the stairwell, into the subway tunnel. I turned back to the street. Focus, I told myself. Focus on the task at hand. I needed to find a turkey. On this island of four million people, there had to be a turkey.

As I walked towards Sixth Avenue, I felt a hand grip my shoulder. Hard. I turned around.

"What the hell were you doing in there?" said Haejin. She was standing on the street alone. Her face was red.

"Where are your parents?"

"Heading back to their hotel room," she said. "Who were you with?"

"Why do you care all of a sudden?" I felt foolish as soon as I said it. "Just a client," I said. "Pro bono."

"She looked like some slut you picked up from the street."

"That's the cruellest thing I have ever heard you say."

Haejin seemed to break out of her fury. Her eyes, hard this whole time, softened. "I just can't believe you followed me."

"I can't believe you won't introduce me to your parents."

"They are traditional," said Haejin, letting out a sigh that spanned the centuries. "I can't introduce you just as a boyfriend. Introducing a guy to your parents is serious."

"I proposed!"

"But we're not engaged."

"Whose fault is that?"

She looked at me as if struck by an inspiration, a look she sometimes got when she had an idea for a new painting. As we walked up Sixth Avenue, she kept her eyes level, her face an expression of equanimity.

"Your parents could do a lot worse than me," I said.

"How's that?"

"I'm a New York lawyer. I've paid off all my student loans. I'm not even thirty."

"You're a dream come true."

"Their dreams, at least," I said. "If not yours."

Haejin winced. "Maybe not," she said. "Maybe your people and mine don't mix."

"What, artists and lawyers?" I said. "We've been through this already." I had already explained to Haejin that just because I was a lawyer didn't mean I lacked an aesthetic sensibility, or that law itself didn't have creative elements, and anyway, what was wrong with being logical? She could use a bit more logic herself.

"It's not that," she said.

"What then, it's because I'm a Namer?"

"My parents are extremely traditional."

"I grew up a few blocks away from their shop. I'm practically their homie!"

"Vietnamese people are not really Confucian," she said.

"What?"

"I researched it."

"You and your research," I said. Haejin would get this way. Spend a month reading up on a topic and start developing ideas.

"Confucianism was only introduced to Vietnam through Chinese rule. At heart, you have a different set of values."

"And those are?"

She did not answer, though I had become truly curious. I continued walking north.

"You should go back to your parents," I said. "I need to find a turkey."

"My parents are going to see the Empire State Building. They don't need me there. I'll help you."

"You've suddenly changed your mind about something?"

"No," she said. "But I feel responsible. I mean, for the turkey."

She was in fact responsible. This was Thanksgiving weekend, Canadian Thanksgiving, *our* Thanksgiving. A bunch of us expats had committed ourselves to getting together the next day at a friend's apartment in Brooklyn for a real home-cooked meal, more than a month earlier than everyone else on this island. Just to forget all the craziness. Haejin had originally volunteered to get the turkey. Then she started flaking out about her parents' visit, so I said I would get it.

If a turkey was to be found, it would be at a supermarket like Gristedes. We walked up and down the aisles of the poultry section looking for the big bird.

"If I was Japanese," I said, "maybe I could understand this aversion, since they colonized your Korean asses."

"That is true."

"But the Namers were colonized by the Japanese too. For a little while. And you already know about the Chinese. For like a thousand years."

"We were never colonized by the Chinese."

"Well, you know what I mean."

Along the aisles we found duck, we found chicken, but we could find no turkey. I felt incensed. I walked up to one of the clerks.

"Where are the turkeys?"

"You mean the Butterballs? They're in storage. Off-site."

"What gives?"

"Saving them for Thanksgiving, next month."

"It is Thanksgiving," I said. "*Our* Thanksgiving."

"It's not your Thanksgiving, or anyone's Thanksgiving," he said.

Before I could reply, Haejin led me out by the arm.

"We should just get a capon," she said. "It's a large chicken. The meat will taste just about the same."

"A capon is not a turkey," I said. "We made a commitment."

I kept walking. We scoured the grocery stores, butcher shops, and bodegas of Midtown, walking the wide avenues and criss-crossing the smaller streets. Haejin came with me. At first she was frustrated by my stubbornness, but as we walked, the frustration turned to a practised indifference, and as the hours passed, she and I both succumbed to the enchantment of the city's skyline.

At times our hands brushed and our fingers lingered together, though they never locked. All this walking reminded me of when we had first come to this city a year earlier, together but for separate reasons, me to the law firm, Haejin to pursue her painting while working at galleries. We would wander the streets for hours, without destination, on the vague premise of familiarizing ourselves with the city, knowing with each turn of a corner that this would be an infinite task.

"Haejin," I said when we stopped by the tall trees of Bryant Park, "are you still thinking about that email?"

One of Haejin's friends had died a few months earlier, and Haejin had sent out an email about it. I was in a warehouse in Wisconsin on a document review and didn't respond. I was one of about two dozen recipients, and might have been on the cc line. I didn't ask about her friend until I was back in New York a couple of weeks later. I was surprised when Haejin blew up at me. You didn't even bother to ask how I was doing, she said. You sent a mass email, I said. I didn't want to clog up your inbox with another "So sorry, boo hoo." He was one of my best friends, she said. Then why didn't you tell me if you cared about what I thought? I did tell you. No, like personally.

"No," she said. "Not anymore."

Daylight turned to evening, and by the time we backtracked our way to Park Avenue, to the Swissôtel, we had been rejected by every store we had walked into.

"Now what?" I said.

"Take a nap. Things will get clearer with some rest." Haejin followed me to the hotel lobby, then to the elevator banks.

"You're not following me up to my room, are you?"

"My feet hurt," she said. "I want to take my shoes off for a bit."

...

Haejin took off more than her shoes. Afterwards, we sat in the dark on my bed, and I again asked her to marry me. She said, again, that she would think about it.

Haejin got up and looked out the window. She wouldn't let me turn on any of the lights, so as not to dilute the skyline. The view faced south.

"I used to look for the Towers," she said. "Just to get my bearings."

"So did everyone," I said. "Just like I did the ski slopes at Grouse Mountain at night."

"Me too."

I stood up next to her. I had no idea what time in the night it was when the phone rang. It was the hotel lobby again.

"It's your wife's husband," said the concierge.

"That makes absolutely no sense," I said. Before I could finish my thought, the phone hung up. I turned on the lights and told Haejin to put on her clothes quick.

Someone was knocking on the door, although there

was a buzzer. When I opened it, there was a man my height, but about a third skinnier. He was wearing a red shirt that matched his bloodshot eyes, with an Amoco badge over his heart. He carried on him a strong smell of gasoline.

"Where is my wife?" he said in Vietnamese. I cocked my head, pretending that I did not understand him. Then he said Nga's name.

"I don't know where she is," I said.

"You are her lawyer?" he said, this time in English. "She told me that she hired a lawyer."

I nodded my head. "Hire is a bit of an overstatement," I said. "I'm helping her for free."

He stepped into the room. Then he grabbed me by the arms, lifted me, and pinned me against the wall as though I were a mirror to be hung.

"Where is she?" he said. "You have to let me know where she is."

"I have no idea," I said, stunned by being lifted off my feet by a man who was slighter than I was.

"Let him go," said Haejin, standing behind this man. He ignored her.

"Where are you hiding her?" he said to me. Then he screwed up his eyes and said in Vietnamese: "You're a Northerner, aren't you? You have that high nose."

"Yes," I said in Vietnamese.

The man bared his teeth and curled his nostrils as if he had just smelled the gasoline off his own skin.

"No," I said. "I mean, I am Canadian—not that type

of Northerner." Then I switched to English: "I can assure you, I'm not hiding her anywhere. Now please put me down."

His arms eased and I drifted to the floor. I straightened the collar of the dress shirt I was wearing. He took a deep breath. His eyes were moistening. "Did she tell you she no longer loves me?" I resisted the urge to put my hand on his shoulder to comfort him.

"She didn't say that," I said. "I'm sure she still loves you."

"Then what did she tell you?"

"What she tells me is privileged," I said. "Most of it, anyway. Well, I can say that she thinks that you've been abusive, and that she needs to leave you."

"Not true!" he said. "Absolutely not true!" He wiped his eyes, then looked at me as if he was suffering some sort of revelation. Then he balled his hand into a fist, took a step back, cocked his fist. I had just enough time to raise my hands to my face.

Then I heard a yell, a low, guttural sound, but it didn't come from Nga's husband. Before he did anything to me, Haejin jumped on his back, knocking him forward. He tripped over my shoe and hit his head against the wall. Hard. He lay on the ground motionless, his hands over his head.

"I have no idea what I just did," said Haejin. There was blood on the carpet. Nga's husband had hit his head on a nail in the wall, for a painting that was no longer there.

"Get some ice from the hallway," I said. "There's a bucket on the table."

While Haejin went out to the hallway, Nga's husband pulled himself up from the floor, a hand on his forehead. Blood was dripping down the side of his face to his shirt.

"I'm sorry," I said.

"I'm okay," he said. "No problem."

Haejin came back with the ice and found a first aid kit. Nga's husband cleaned himself up, and I gave him one of my laundered shirts. The fit was perfect. Then he sat on my bed, put his hands on his knees, and closed his eyes.

"Please, tell me where my wife is," he said. "I am so worried."

"He's not going anywhere until you tell him," said Haejin.

"I should call security."

"I think he's been roughed up enough. Do you have any idea where she is?"

"Even if I did, I'm her lawyer."

"This has nothing to do with the law," said Haejin. "It's his wife. He looks worried sick."

Haejin at least had one point: if I was to get this man out of my hotel room peaceably, I would have to give him what he wanted.

"I have only one idea," I told him. I put on my jacket, Haejin put on hers, and we walked out.

The man followed us down to the number 6 train. I took him to the only place that I could think of. By now it was the middle of the night, and New York was a netherworld. We got out at Astor Place to an empty scene, then headed again towards Broadway. You could actually hear the rustle of fallen leaves. Manhattan had disappeared, replaced by a ghost town.

...

We walked down the same flight of stairs I had walked down earlier that day (or was it the day before?). I was going to tell Nga's husband that this was where Nga had taken me earlier in the day, that I had no idea where else she would be, and that he could wait here until she returned, whenever that might be. I had expected a metal grate to be drawn over the gallery's window, like so many shops in New York. The last thing I expected was a light to be on inside.

"Someone's there," said Haejin. The glow from the window illuminated her breath.

Nga's husband banged on the door in the manner that he had at my hotel room. No one came. He twisted the doorknob and it opened.

We walked into the broad gallery space. There, in the centre of the space, was Nga. She had a brush in her hand, hunched over a lacquer painting. She looked at me, then her husband.

"I'm sorry," she said in Vietnamese. "I had to finish this. I felt inspired."

I walked up to the painting. "There goes your affidavit," I said. The landscape looked familiar. "What is it?"

"Burns Bog," said Nga. "As I remember it."

"We should leave them alone," said Haejin.

"Not until I know whether I still have a client."

"Let's go outside at least," said Haejin.

Haejin and I stood on the sidewalk like sentries while Nga and her husband talked inside. It was sunrise. The city began to swell with people and cars. Haejin went across the street to get us coffees.

We must have been there for over an hour when Nga opened the door of the gallery. "You should go home," she said.

"Are we still making the affidavit?" I said.

She didn't answer, just looked sad and contrite. "You must be so tired," she said. "We'll speak soon." She closed the door.

Back on the street, I said to Haejin, "We still don't have a turkey." Our friends would be gathering at the apartment in Brooklyn in the early afternoon. "We might as well go home and get a couple of hours of sleep."

"We've made it this far," said Haejin. "Why don't we just keep going?"

...

Haejin and I walked south, past the site where the Towers had stood, beyond the lingering mourners at St. Paul's Chapel, and over the Brooklyn Bridge, holding hands. We took the whole morning. We didn't bother looking for a turkey. We arrived at the apartment surrounded by our friends, all of whom had moved here from all over our country. They had everything ready for me and Haejin laid out on the kitchen table — the stuffing for the turkey made out of apples and maple syrup in a big red bowl, the cranberry sauce still in tins. Haejin covered her eyes when she saw the baster lying expectantly next to the empty roasting pan lined with foil. I wanted to cover my eyes as well, but it was up to me to speak the simple truth: "We couldn't find a turkey. We didn't bring anything."

Haejin and I couldn't face each other for the rest of the meal. Our friends, though, were understanding. We rifled through takeout menus. We gorged on stuffing as if we were the turkey. One of us broke a box of Smarties open into a glass bowl, then broke open another. Haejin and I were separated, lost to each other among our friends and in their warm embraces. We almost forgot what we had escaped, what had escaped us.

Toad Poem

Diem knew that one day he would return to Hoi An to write his toad poem—to memorialize his parents in verse so great as to rouse the heavens from indifference. Forty-five years ago, he had fled Vietnam at the age of nineteen by merchant ship, making it to the Philippines, then Vancouver. There he had stayed put all these years, until the day he emptied his meagre life savings from a CIBC account and boarded an Asiana flight to Da Nang, connecting through Seoul. He bought a suit for the trip. The young officers at the airport in Da Nang leered at his shiny grey suit, his canary-yellow tie, and his Canadian passport and visa, and asked him in English if he was travelling alone. When Diem answered in Vietnamese that he was indeed alone, they asked him (stubbornly administering their broken English) for his "purpose." "Simply pleasure," Diem said in Vietnamese, and the officers checked his visa again, then for a third time, and finally let him through.

Diem had intended to take a bus to Hoi An, but a skinny young man wearing a baseball cap snatched his suitcase the moment he put it down, smiling at Diem then walking away. If Diem had been younger, he would have run the man down and cracked his spine with his fist. But as it was, he could only follow limply. It was too early in this trip to start crying for the help of strangers. Although the man kept up a brisk pace, he had no intention of outrunning Diem, and Diem followed him through sliding glass doors out into the warm, damp night air that felt suddenly so familiar. The man stopped at a green taxicab with an open trunk.

"Da Nang?" asked the man.

Diem shook his head.

"Cheaper than a bus," said the man in English, placing the luggage into the trunk.

"Hoi An," said Diem, and got into the back seat.

The man tried to ply Diem with conversation in broken English, and when Diem did not answer, the man switched to broken Mandarin. Diem replied in the languid central Vietnamese accent, and the cab driver turned to face Diem with one hand still gripping the steering wheel while the other hovered over the horn. He did not ask where Diem had come from, only asked if he wanted a driver for the next day.

"I'll take you to all the sights," said the driver in Vietnamese. "The ruins of My Son, the ruins of My Lai. Even Hue, if you have the time. Cheap."

"No, thank you," said Diem. "I'm not a tourist."

The man dropped him off at the five-star hotel that Diem had booked across the river from Hoi An's Old Town.

By ten the next morning, Diem was wearing the same suit and tie and strolling the Old Town, feeling as if he had fallen back to earth after a lifetime away. To Diem's surprise, he was perspiring. The locals were unperturbed in long sleeves, some even wore jackets, and here he was like the many tourists — red-faced like the Koreans or Australians fanning themselves with open copies of their Rough Guides.

He walked the north-south streets of the Old Town where American sailors on break from the local patrol boat base once walked arm in arm, haphazardly bartering. Back then, Hoi An was not a UNESCO World Heritage Site and he did not have to buy a ticket to enter the Old Town. Here were the merchant houses that he had taken refuge in while hiding from a war that was happening everywhere, it seemed, except here. Somehow, by some guiding hand, Hoi An was spared despite being in the centre of the country, close to the DMZ. These houses were elegant mutts of Vietnamese, Chinese, Japanese, and even French architecture, built in the centuries before the Thu Bon River silted up and turned this trading post of a city into a museum piece, preserved in the amber sunlight. Some of the houses had wide facades with colonial balconies, but also dragon-scale rooftops made from yin-yang tiles. The Japanese elements were in the triple beams descending from the ceilings and, to Diem, in the houses' nighttime air of secrecy, when the facades were enclosed by black wooden shutters slotted one on top of another.

What, then, was truly Vietnamese about any of this? The answer lay in the mornings, when the shutters were lifted off and each house became an open storefront with limpid bartering or gossip beneath its awning—in the way that private lives were open to street view. It was in the tropical moss, glistening green along the walls that were painted to shine like yellow sandstone in the afternoons. It was in the incense that was lit in the early evening by the shopkeepers to venerate the ancestors, before the shopkeepers boarded up the front again. At least this was how he remembered it.

When Diem was a young man, the merchant houses were dilapidated, the roofs sagging, the shutters of the facades cracked, coal-scorched, and ancient. Now the roofs had been restored and the shutters painted with this lacquered sheen, as if honey had been poured over them. The stores were now chic boutiques, no longer doubling as homes or echoing with bartering. Even the tendrils of moss along the walls seemed finely articulated.

He had rehearsed many times over what he would do if someone called out to him as he walked down Nguyen Thai Hoc Street as he was doing now. The merchant who gave him refuge, for instance, or the shopkeepers he met that spring. How he would explain himself. No, he would say, he did not come back with a wife and descendants, and yet his life had been successful nonetheless. But after an hour of walking, he met no one he recognized. Diem was sure that Mr. Fang, the old merchant, was long departed. The tourists who towered above him dodged him as if he were a post in the dirt. To the young locals he was a pane of glass. Maybe the locals were instructed to ignore his ilk. None of them asked where he had come from or what he had been up to all these years. Their chatter, either eye to eye or into a phone, was painfully clear and bright to Diem, so full of their own concerns and the life of this alien place.

He found a fancy-looking restaurant with little palm trees set in planters, and retreated to its rear patio — to get away from the people on the street as much as anything. The patio was mostly empty, except for a waitress clearing the dirty plates and glasses that remained on the tables.

The waitress smiled when she saw him, but said in English that they would not be open for another hour.

"That's fine, I'll wait," he answered in Vietnamese. "Let an old man rest here awhile." He realized that she was likely clearing dishes from a banquet the night before.

She seemed surprised that he spoke Vietnamese, and showed him a table. "Would you like some water?" she said.

"How about a beer fresh?" he said, and the waitress complied, then started clearing the table next to him. She would be his daughter's age, if he had one. In fact the waitress was dressed exactly like so many young women back in Vancouver would be right now, on a drizzly mid-spring day — in trousers and a light cashmere sweater that was rolled up to her elbows. Yes, just like his daughter, he thought. Except for the blue-green tattoo of raindrops in a strange pattern that this waitress sported on her wrist. He would never allow his daughter to have a tattoo.

He asked the waitress for a napkin. She got him one and just smiled as though he were from China, then returned to clearing and resetting tables. It awed him to see her move so swiftly from under one umbrella to another, without breaking a sweat in the sweltering heat.

He tore the napkin in half, used one half to wipe his face and the other to write on. He needed to figure out how long he could live in Vietnam with the traveller's cheques he had stowed in his room's safe.

"Excuse me, miss," he said to the waitress, then pulled on the back of her sweater, because she did not seem to hear him. She turned around with a stack of dishes in her arms, tried to re-affix her smile for him, although now it was lopsided.

"Do you know where I can find the exchange rates?" he asked.

"Are you asking about the wifi?" she said. "Yes, we certainly have wifi."

"No," he said. "Where is the bank? They'll have the exchange rates there."

She looked at him quizzically. "What are you exchanging?"

"Dollars for dong," he said. "Canadian dollars."

"Oh, that's easy," said the waitress. "It's one Canadian dollar to 19,300 dong. Give or take."

"How do you know that?"

"We have many customers from Canada," said the waitress.

He wrote down these mind-boggling numbers on his napkin. Earlier in the morning he had stopped by the covered market to look at the price of food and clothing. Now he regarded his half-drunk beer fresh, which cost fifty cents. He made a few educated guesses about the price of a room, if not in the Old Town then perhaps in the surrounding villages, somewhere the tourists never went, where the locals lived on less than three thousand dollars a year. He looked over the results of his initial calculations, and tore up his napkin.

He started his calculations over. He would not have long even if he stayed in a thatched hut with a pounded mud floor, a few months at most. So why bother scrimping? He had scrimped his whole life and had little more than a bag of bones to show for it. At fifty dollars a night he might as well extend his hotel reservation. Why prolong his poverty when he could spend a much shorter time in luxury?

"Miss, come here," he said.

"I'll be right over after I clean up this table."

"Has this country changed so much?" he said to her. "Is it no longer rude to ignore your elders?"

The waitress came over, carrying a pile of dishes in her arms. "Yes, how can I help you, sir?"

"Another napkin, please," he said. Then he took out a bill from his wallet—from the large wad of American bills that he had saved for street beggars — and handed it to her. "For your time," he said.

The waitress took the bill and nodded solemnly. "Are you working on more exchange rates?" said the waitress. "I can tell you the conversion for American dollars to dong, if you'd like."

"I've had enough of numbers," he said. Now he wanted to start on his toad poem. "Miss, do you know the old story, about the toad poem?" he said. She was about to turn away, so he took another bill from his wallet and gave it to her.

"No, it's not something we learned in school," she said, pocketing the bill.

"Are you serious? Your parents never told you?"

"I lost my parents when I was very young."

"I'm sorry to hear that. That must explain the tattoo on your wrist. You didn't have parents to teach you the proper ways."

The waitress looked at the pattern on her wrist. "No, it's just beautiful," she said.

"The last time I was in this country, only gangsters and criminals wore tattoos. Never mind girls. Never mind respectable girls!"

She squinted at him the way certain women did back in Vancouver on the bus, when they found him peeking over their shoulders to see what they were reading. Perhaps it was just the sun. "And what about your parents?" she asked.

Diem choked on the mention of his parents, and had to take a sip of his beer fresh.

"Oh, my father was the richest man in our village," said Diem, though his answer didn't seem complete. "He owned the village's only machine-operated rice mill. He was friends with all the Chinese merchants in Da Nang and Hoi An." Diem would in fact come to owe his life to one of his father's merchant connections. "But my father liked to think of himself as a man of the people."

"I know quite a few men like that," said the waitress. "They are all members of the Party."

Diem spat on the ground. "Do not mention my father in the same breath as those people," he said.

"Dear heavens," said the waitress, looking at the spittle on the ground. "I didn't know people still did that."

Diem bent down to wipe the spittle, and when he got up, he gave her another bill.

"And my mother," said Diem, struggling for the right words. "She was from Hue, at least before she moved to my father's village," he continued. "So she ran our home like it was the imperial court." He hemmed and hawed for more words.

"You mentioned the toad poem?" said the waitress.

"Oh, yes," said Diem, grateful to her for returning to his subject. "A toad poem is from the old folk tale about four idiot poets getting drunk at a tavern."

"I should have known," said the waitress.

"One of them saw our proverbial toad by a stand of

trees and was inspired to belch out the following verse: 'What a small toad, just resting in the shadows.'"

"How fascinating," said the waitress, though she had turned her back to Diem now, and resumed cleaning up the table beside him.

"There's more to it," said Diem. When the waitress turned around, he gave her another bill. "Seeing the toad stir, the next poet said: 'What a small toad, now hopping out of the shadows.' When the toad came to rest, the third idiot contributed: 'There it goes now, out into the open, and now once again it is resting.' The fourth poet, watching the toad, finished the poem: 'There it stays now, not a single shiver. And now there it goes again, hopping away!'"

"Of course, course," said the waitress. "Would you like more beer fresh?"

"No, you don't see," said Diem. "The story isn't finished yet." He gave her another bill before she could walk away. "In fact, the puzzle is with what happens next: After reciting the poem, the idiots became quite sombre. They feared, you see, that they had angered the heavens with a creation of such audacious beauty that they would be struck dead. And so they ordered four coffins, placing the order through the tavern keeper. The punchline doesn't matter—the tavern keeper asked what the fuss was all about, and then the poets recited the complete poem. After, the tavern keeper ordered five coffins—the poem was in fact so awful that the tavern keeper feared he too would die from having the idiots repeat it!"

"Bravo," said the waitress, though she wasn't clapping. "Would you like to see our lunch menu? It won't be long now before we open."

"The intended humour of the ending has always eluded me," said Diem. Diem had heard the story as a child, and even now its meaning lay just beyond his grasp. He didn't understand what sort of god begrudged a man's creative impulse. He was brought up Catholic and both his parents believed that all beauty was an expression of God's grace. (His parents were the rare birds in their village because they did not regularly light incense or make offerings at the ancestral altar, preferring instead to recite rosaries before the shrine to the Blessed Virgin and the Infant Jesus of Prague.) Most of the villagers Diem grew up with were Buddhists, though Diem suspected that the algebra of karma would not come down so hard on toad poets. And neither would retribution be warranted under Confucianism. Perhaps the tale had some Taoist origin, but he was not familiar enough with the pantheon of Taoist deities to know if any of them could be moved in such a way by a toad poem.

He reached for his pen, thought better of it, put it back down. "Yes, I'll have a menu," he said.

The waitress came back with something that didn't look like a menu at all; it was leather-bound with black tassels, and looked as though it belonged at the entrance to a wedding reception.

"For an orphan, you're doing quite well for yourself," he said. "But you can do better." He held out another bill, but this time she only looked at it, then at him, squinting again. Finally she took the bill.

"Did your government train you to bite your tongue before taking money from foreigners?" he asked. He truly wanted to know. "It must be a useful skill, dealing with so many belligerent tourists."

The waitress turned her back to him again, and he could tell from the heaving of her shoulders that she was taking deep breaths, composing herself.

"Well?" he said.

She turned to face him. "I learned my patience from my parents," she said. "They met during the war, on the Ho Chi Minh trail. That's where I was born, somewhere along the trail."

"Dear heavens," said Diem. "Soldiers shouldn't have babies in the middle of a war."

"They carried shovels instead of guns," said the waitress. "They were the ones who spent the night fixing the parts of the road that the Americans bombed the day before. I remember sitting on the edges of the roads, watching. I never thought about it then, I was only five or six, but I can't believe how patient they were, shovelling side by side when another bomb could drop on them at any time. One day it did."

"I see," said Diem.

"I don't remember much about my parents," she said, "but I do remember their perseverance. I owe my life to them, of course, but not only that." She gestured to the sunlit world around them, the tasselled menu, the potted palm trees. "I owe *this* life to them. We all do."

The waitress smiled widely at Diem now, baring her imperfect teeth and the crow's feet around her eyes. She was, in fact, somewhat older than he had thought.

"Yes," said Diem, and although thoughts were welling up in his mind from what she had just said, he could not find the words for them. "Um, I think I will order now."

Other customers were now finding the patio. He turned to the menu, which was ostensibly Vietnamese but with touches of international flair to jack the prices up. Pho noodles with wagyu beef or braised chicken with organically grown Chinese ginger. That sort of thing. He ordered the most expensive item.

A different waitress brought him the food, an older woman with a frayed ponytail and too much mascara. Diem must have looked at her with open confusion, because she said, in English, "The other waitress is busy with customers."

"It doesn't matter," he said in Vietnamese. He chewed on tiny, limp vegetables and some sort of crab dish with the traditional *nuoc mam* fish dipping sauce on the side, fortified by a cognac infusion. Diem pushed his half-eaten plate away. Vietnamese cuisine was meant to be comfort food. If it was fancy and expensive, it was not Vietnamese.

"I'm sorry," said the older waitress. "The food did not suit you?"

"I've been away a long time now," answered Diem. "My stomach wants simple fare."

The waitress smiled and brought him the bill. He was surprised that she neither recoiled nor betrayed any further curiosity towards him. He was, after all, an exile from the war and therefore the enemy come home. He tipped the old waitress generously even though she smiled right through him while looking up at the other customers who were starting to come in.

He returned to the streets. It was time to proceed to his intended destination, with no further distraction. He walked by the same type of chic boutiques that he had seen earlier in the day—or was he simply retracing his steps? He wasn't sure. Everything was both repetitive and strange, and he needed something familiar to anchor him to this earth. It was possible that there was someone from his past in the crowd, but time would have worn both of them down beyond recognition. His sun-shrivelled peasant relatives, for instance. And despite decades in the cloud-world of Vancouver, when Diem had seen his reflection in the hotel that morning, he could not imagine what he had looked like as a young man. He had a fair but lined face from years standing out in the cold rain in Vancouver, from nights patrolling construction sites as a security guard. They were building condos all over Vancouver and its suburbs, and his job was to make sure no one made off with the equipment that the crew left overnight, to shoo away squatters. Years of night rain dripping off the sides of his baseball cap and down his cheeks would do just as well to rut the skin as sunlight.

But no, there was likely no one left who would recognize him anyway. They would have all passed on to the spirit world, if such existed. His mother was strict on these matters — there was a heaven and a hell and that was that. His father's Catholicism was touched by a Vietnamese enchantment — where spirits of departed ancestors shared our world, seemed to linger under the branches of every tree. He made peace with his Catholicism by explaining that these earthbound spirits were wandering in purgatory. His father kept a secret altar in the house as a temporary haven for those who died without any loved ones to honour them with incense and offerings. There were many wandering spirits from the wars, and the living feared them.

Now he walked past demonstrations of ancient folk games that he didn't recall seeing before. Just then, Diem saw something out of the corner of his eye, something uncertainly familiar. It was as if God had turned Diem's musings into a prayer and answered it. Something familiar about a man lying on a hammock in the middle of this street of quaint boutiques, calling out to Diem, his face covered by a bright-red cap. The cap.

"Hello, hello!" said the man. It was the cab driver. Diem stood helplessly as the man rolled out of his hammock and skipped towards him. Hadn't they swept out the bums and their makeshift hammocks by now? thought Diem, before realizing that it was a boutique selling fancy crochet hammocks with spiderweb edgings.

"Are you fed up with this town yet?" asked the man. Diem recognized him by his crisply persistent voice and the cap with the Manchester United logo. This was the first time that Diem could make out the man's face (a boy, really) — the flat nose and wide eyes that narrowed dramatically when he smiled, the swell of the cheeks.

"I've just started to walk," said Diem.

"You shouldn't have to walk," said the man in a respectful, hushed tone that brightened Diem's spirits. His name was Duc.

"I can walk just fine, thank you."

Duc looked him up and down, pausing to admire his tie. "Where did you come from?" he asked.

At last. Someone had finally asked Diem the question that he had been waiting for.

"Vancouver, British Columbia, Canada."

As Diem expected, Duc's eyes lit up. "So many of my friends have moved there."

"No doubt."

"They seem to be doing well."

Diem waited for a remark on Diem's own prosperity, but Duc said nothing more.

"Of course they are," Diem said finally. "You know, I was one of the first in Vancouver. It was not much back then." Without realizing it, Diem was pointing at his own chest.

"I'd like to visit."

"Just visit?"

"To see the forests," said Duc. "I hear you can drink the rain. And the fresh air. I hear that you can smell the forest inside the city."

"Fresh air and clean rain. Simple tastes." That's why he was stuck in this country chasing after petty fares, thought Diem. "There's something else you may not have thought of," said Diem. "Over there, there are not so many wandering spirits haunting everyone."

"Really?" said Duc. "That sounds wonderful. I'm always on my tiptoes here, looking over my shoulder. I don't sleep well at night, especially. Only during the day."

"I understand how that is, son," said Diem. Sometimes Diem thought that he had fled Vietnam simply to escape those spirits. He slept much better in Vancouver, and credited the spiritlessness of the place. Almost spirit-less. Diem believed that one soul had made it across the Pacific with him on the merchant ship, that of a departed aunt who had tailed Diem all over Vancouver, chiding him over his chronic bachelorhood. In Vietnam he had had many admirers among the village girls, but in Vancouver he was largely ignored. During a Kitsilano bar-hopping phase in the early eighties he would leave the establishments empty-handed and hear his aunt's voice through the rustling maple leaves, spreading from star to star in the night ("You can't just sit for them to come to you. You are the man. You are the tiger on the hunt, not them!"). He sidled up to women on bar stools then froze after trying to introduce himself, as much from the prospect of his aunt's ridicule as from trying to charm a lady through his thick accent and partially real-ized *Nature of Things* moustache. By the time Canada's constitution was repatriated from Britain, he had shorn his bristles and given up on women.

"I can take you to the beach nearby," said Duc. "Cheap. China Beach is nice even at night."

"Thank you, but I'll stay here."

Duc nodded graciously and watched Diem disappear into the crowd. He could be some dispatch of the Communist authorities tasked with tailing him, for all Diem knew. As Diem proceeded along Nguyen Thai Hoc Street, past the buzzing zithers of traditional music, he thought he could see the red cap flit in and out of his peripheral vision.

Now Diem made his way to Hoang Dieu Street, so different from what it was in the 1960s. The buildings had been restored to the Politburo's vision of eight-eenth-century grandeur, except for the global brand names sprouting from storefronts. There were also more antique lanterns festooning the buildings now. His soul burrowed into his chest. He feared walking to the end of the street and not finding what he was looking for.

But there it was, the third-to-last storefront — Mr. Fang's tailor shop. The oriental lanterns over the awnings were a new touch, but there was the same announcement in Chinese carved into a wooden banister, the same single elevated step onto the brick floor where silk dresses beckoned. He knew he would not find Mr. Fang inside, nor likely his spirit, since this shop was just a minor occupation for Mr. Fang, one of his many business interests. Forty-five years ago it was run by his daughter.

A young woman greeted Diem with a plastic water bottle and a small white towel. Inside, he pressed the towel against his eyes to soften the sting of memory. It was the same parquet floor with potted ferns and red lanterns hanging from the ceilings, the same teak panelling and mannequins arranged around the floor in dark suits and evening dresses—an eternal cocktail hour for headless colonials.

"How may I help you?" she said in English.

There is nothing you can do, he wanted to say. Instead, he answered in English: "Are you the owner of this store?"

The woman shook her head, then smiled and covered her teeth with a hand. "Oh, you are Vietnamese!" she said, and switched to their native tongue. "I can tell by your accent."

Diem cowered in his suit, could feel the presence of his aunt behind him. "Is Miss Fang still here?"

"I don't know of a Miss Fang," said the woman. "Madame Nguyen owns this store."

"Well, then, is she here?"

"I can check. Do you have a message?"

"I'm just an old customer." Diem's throat was dry and he took a sip of the water. Left alone, he drifted past the mannequins in bespoke dress towards a smaller space in the back, where bolts of uncut silk lined wooden shelves. The smell had always jarred him. The silk was smooth as ice, the colours so bright and liquid, yet it all smelled of fish.

He felt a whisper on the back of his neck, and he turned to see a woman in crisp white trousers and a green striped shirt (silk, of course) with flaring collars. She hadn't changed, not really. Yes, her face was lined, her pallor bone-white, but that simply accentuated her beauty, the high cheekbones and diamond chin that was a Vietnamese birthright, her large, coal-black eyes now set in stark relief. She looked all the more elegant for not trying to stand in the way of Time. The surprising difference, if any, was with her hair, not the white streaks but rather how it ended in a bob around the shoulders. It used to be much longer.

She offered her hand, palm down as if it was something steady to hold on to. "Can I help you?" she said.

He took her hand briefly, just to test reality. She did not introduce herself, nor did she ask Diem for his name. She did not mention that her father had once hid Diem in the attic of this shop.

She was an obedient daughter, had come up to the attic to leave Diem food on days when the tailor couldn't do so. The first time she saw him up there, she seemed confused by this lanky son of a wealthy village elder hiding out like some common refugee. Diem had, in fact, deserted his South Vietnamese army squad while it was passing near his family's village on its way to the central highlands. Desertion was not uncommon among ragtag draftees, who were sent to the battlefields without knowing how to fire an M-16. His orientation had taken place in what seemed like a converted school near Hue, sitting cross-legged and listening to a sergeant read passages from a US Army training manual without ever lifting his head.

Diem was a deserter, but he was no coward, leaving more out of hunger than fear. He was a willing draftee without knowing how the hunger would eat at him. After three months he was sick of the vacuum-packed rations of rice and soy sauce they distributed, which he suspected were US Army leftovers from the Korean War. He never planned to run away. The M35 truck was driving at night near his village, and he knew the lay of the jungle and paddies blindfolded. When he jumped through an opening in the canvas cargo cover, he heard only laughter; his superiors thought it was just another private falling out of the back of the deuce-and-a-half after nodding off. The truck didn't even slow down. They assumed he would run after it, but instead he disappeared into the forest. He just wanted a home-cooked meal.

"I'd like a suit."

She tapped her tongue against her lip. She seemed taller, but really it was just his stoop against her perfect posture.

"A special occasion?" she asked, taking out her measuring tape. She didn't ask him where he had come from.

He did not recall if he had ever told her he was headed to Canada before that night when he escaped from Vietnam.

Once, sometime before he fled the country, she had invited him downstairs for lunch. The store was closed for the midday siesta and her father was gone. They had known each other for a month, and by now she was sneaking magazines and novels up to him. They sat at a table in the small courtyard in the middle of the house. The table was lit by a spotlight of sun almost directly above them, and they were surrounded by the shadows and silhouettes of old teak furniture. It was hot and she acted bored, letting her *cao lau* noodles sit in their shallow broth while she stared into the gloom. From somewhere in the back came the muted hum of sewing machines. They might have talked about a novel she had lent him.

After lunch she said he could nap in the living room, which was cooler than the stifling attic. When he woke up, the house seemed empty. He turned a corner, trying to find the stairway back to the attic. Instead, he found a room with thin curtains draped on the far end, against which an indiscernible silhouette was thrown up from a dim light on the other side. Then the silhouette disappeared. He walked towards the curtains, found an opening, and stepped into a pool of steam and refracted light coming from a corner. She was standing in the dark, naked, or mostly so, looking out a small opening of sunlight through another set of curtains, a book in her hand that caught the light, sweat on the soft side of her wrist. Her hair went past her shoulders, maybe wet, but he wasn't sure. She looked at him with a sealed smile, her eyes half-closed as if she had forgotten her nakedness, or as if he was a simpleton and it didn't matter. He excused himself, found his way back to the stairs with his hands. That was the closest he had ever come to experiencing the supernatural. Later, she laughed at him for pretending the moment had never happened. "You were asleep," she said. "So I picked up a *roman*."

Now she told him to take off his blazer and tie and slid the tape measure down his arm.

"I'm visiting my parents' village," he said.

"Your parents?"

"Their souls, really."

"Of course."

"I'm from Canada," he said, as if to explain why he had not seen his parents while they were still alive.

"I can tell that you are not from around here, at least not for some time."

He smiled. At last a hint of recognition. Playing strangers was just her game.

He teased her. "I'm here to write a poem," he said.

"You don't need a suit for that."

"A toad poem."

"I see. So you need a suit for your coffin."

"You know, I could never understand the ending of that story."

"All the folk tales come from a seed of truth," she said.

"Think of all the poets who died young. It's more romantic to say that it was heaven's price for genius, isn't it?"

"Than what?"

"Than reality. That poets usually die from being crazy, poor, or drunk."

"I'm not crazy," said Diem. "I'm not really a poet."

She smiled. "I didn't mean that."

He put a finger on one of the wooden rods on which the silk bolts hung, and his finger drifted down rod to rod. He chose the black silk, because it struck his eye among all the vibrant colour.

"You're taking this seriously," she said. She measured his dimensions, it seemed to Diem, not for his suit but for his coffin. He held his breath when her face drew near his as she wrapped the tape around his collar, and he thought about what his life could have been.

"The shirt you are wearing is much too large," she said. "We can alter it as well, no charge." She told him to unbutton his shirt, and he could try on a replacement in the meantime.

"Another thing," she said, whispering in his ear, "the colour of your belt should match the colour of your shoes. It's the little things that spell success."

She placed a bunch of pins between her lips and began marking off the sleeves. Diem's cheeks got hot. "Thank you," he said. "This is how I want my parents to see me, as a success."

She spat out the pins. "Do you even know where they are?"

"I'm sure they are in heaven now."

"So no longer in purgatory?"

"I'm sure of that."

She stepped away from him and looked down at her hands. "It's horrible to spend your afterlife wandering aimlessly among strangers, isn't it? Why wouldn't we do everything to save the ones we love?"

"You don't understand," he said. He wiped the spittle from his mouth with the back of his hand. "Of course the Communists would come after the biggest house in the village. They chose their fate. There was nothing for me to do." The buttons of his shirt were undone and his shirt was drunkenly untucked.

"You could have stayed with them."

"To do what? To simply tend to their graves, if I didn't also end up beside them? And then what? I had no wife, no children."

"Your parents' souls are your children," she said. "Their eternal happiness is in your hands."

He nodded, tucked in his shirt, buttoned his sleeves. "I've always kept an altar for them."

She wiped the edge of her lip with a bolt of silk. "You'll have your suit by the end of the day."

"Can I see where you make them?"

"Still curious," she said, then bit her lip. "Okay."

She led him through the familiar arcs of shadow and light towards a humming in the back. She opened a thin plywood door, behind which was a large room where rows of girls in pink hairnets were working with sewing machines. Large electric fans kept generators from over-heating under fluorescent lights speckled with dead flies. Fresh flowers in a tin can reached for a small window.

"Nothing has changed," he said.

"You've been here before?" she asked.

Was she still playing? He stayed silent.

"What's really changed is the cost of electricity," she said. "It's valuable as gold. I heard they are building big dams in Cambodia. Maybe we'll get some of it."

"Cambodian electricity," he said. "Just what this house needs."

She closed the plywood door and muted the sewing machines to a dim hum as they returned to the store. "Where are you staying?" she said. "We can deliver to your hotel." She gave him her card.

He read the card out loud. "Madame Nguyen," he said.

"I'm married now," she whispered, then disappeared. He felt lifted by this confession.

Back out on the streets, he found Duc lying among the fancy hammocks.

"I need a driver."

"Cheap, cheap," Duc tweeted, saluting. They walked together out of the Old Town, stopping by the Japanese covered bridge. To his relief, it was the same old bridge, with its worn tiled roof and brittle wood picket railing, except now he needed a ticket to enter its little shrine.

They found Duc's cab and headed for his parents' village. Diem dreaded what he would find in place of the grand old house, but there was no turning back.

Diem's father liked to call himself a farmer, although he had a courtier's hands — soft, long, and slender. He was the largest landholder in their village, owning four-teen hectares of paddies, and the only one who could afford enough fertilizer to cultivate more fragrant, pre-mium varieties of rice. It was other villagers who bent over to harvest it; his father's tan was from tennis. Diem remembered banquets during the Tet holiday, how his father would end up inviting every single peasant from the village to share in the slaughtered pig, and how his father's dark complexion matched everyone else's, all of them pinkened from rice wine.

Diem's mother was a beautiful but prickly mandarin's daughter from the royal capital of Hue. She liked wearing silk *ao dai* dresses with her hair in a lotus chignon, as if she were attending court, and she never failed to let his father know how much she had sacrificed to be with him. She gave up proximity to family, other Catholics, and all the delicacies of Hue, such as its spicy beef noodles or its royal cuisine garnished with carved mythical creatures. Its solid, weatherproof churches. The way she talked about Hue, it was as if Jesus had been born there. And yet, it seemed to Diem, she was ultimately glad about her sacrifices, glad to walk barefoot in the wet paddy in the early evenings after the workers left, just the three of them, as if they were at a beach resort, for the pleasure of the mud around their ankles, for the feel of coolness in those humid evenings.

Diem had carried in him for years some unwritten

lines about them, like so many pebbles hidden on the floor of his mouth beneath the tongue. All this time he had thought about how easy it would be to write it. Their beautiful, short lives would give ready-made form and momentum to the poem. All he had to do was spit it out.

But now, as the ancient town disappeared behind the cab in a trail of ochre dust, Diem knew that all those errant verses would never cohere into a poem, that the words would die in this pungent air. In the end all he could write down would be the most simple facts of his parents' lives, and that the moments they all shared together were just too brief. They breathed and loved him and each other, he left them, and soon after they were no more.

The Forbidden Purple City

I do not have any appetite for the sentimental music of a bygone era, and so I was leery of picking up the two musicians from the airport. Their youth ran counter to their reputedly stoic commitment to *vong co*, that form of tonal melancholy developed by a Mekong Delta composer almost a hundred years ago. The idea of these dove-cheeked throwbacks frankly smacked of disingenuousness, exploiting our audience's emotional blind spots with old formulas. Tiet Linh booked this husband-and-wife duo for our New Year's concert here in Vancouver, though she was in no state to tend to the details of transportation. She left that to me.

In addition to their luggage, the man carried two hard, black instrument cases, one for him — I thought — and one for her. The couple looked like slick moderns, in their late twenties or early thirties, bleary-eyed from their flight but well dressed and coiffed. Both were over-compensating with wool jackets, knitted caps, scarves, and leather gloves. In fact it rarely ever snows here in Vancouver, though when I led the couple outside into the drizzle they both hugged themselves as if they had underdressed. I admit I was touched by this gesture, perhaps more so than I ever could be by their music. I have lived in Vancouver for over thirty years now, and had forgotten just how cold those first winters were for me. I hurried them into my taxicab, the meter turned off because this was a personal errand.

In my cab we discussed our common connection with Tiet Linh. I didn't ask them about what life was like back in the old country, not even the customary questions about the weather, for though I have not returned in over thirty years, I have gained a sufficient sense of contemporary Vietnam through the internet. Perhaps they took my silence on that matter as an aversion to conversation in general, because for the rest of the ride they kept their chatter to themselves.

"I hope they'll be okay. The air here is very dry," said the man (though, as I have said, it was drizzling).

"You worry about them, and not my throat?" said the woman.

"You can take care of yourself. They can't."

"You shouldn't have brought her. You never listen."

"She's safer with me, even here."

"I wish I felt the same way."

"Don't talk silly."

None of this talk made sense to me at the time, but later I found out that the man was speaking about his *dan bau*, the single-stringed instrument that he kept in one of the cases. The other instrument was an electric moon lute. I know something of the *dan bau*: that when played by a master, the monochrome has the resonance of a woman's vocal cords.

"I will not sing if you play her."

"Don't worry," he said. "She'll stay in the case."

The woman seemed to be comforted by his words, but the peace only lasted for a moment before they started arguing about some point of music theory that I could not grasp. She complained about how he always tried to lose her by playing in *day kep*, the key of the man. He made some fresh retort, and I heard a scratching of plastic that made me worried she was going to fling open the door, but then he said something else that seemed to soothe her.

Perhaps it was disrespectful for them to speak so openly about themselves in the company of an old man, but I didn't mind their self-absorption. Such was their licence as artists, and yes, I also took comfort in listening to the ebbs and flows of a young couple's intimate dispute, as one sometimes does in a sad memory.

I drove them to Tiet Linh's house. The lights of her East Vancouver duplex were off. I was so relieved when her daughter answered the door, but began to worry again when she said that Tiet Linh had retired early. Tiet Linh had become increasingly removed from our affairs ever since Anh Binh, her husband, passed away six months ago.

"Would you like me to leave her a message?" said the daughter.

"Yes, that her guests are here."

"Guests?"

"The musicians that your mother arranged for. All the way from Vietnam. They are staying here, no?"

"Oh, dear," said the daughter, thinking with Anh Binh's darting eyebrows—so much her father's daughter. "Bac Gia, leave the two with me."

I miss Anh Binh dearly for all he did for me over the years, but despite my mourning I am still living up to my responsibilities to ensure the success of the New Year's celebrations. Am I selfish for wishing that Tiet Linh would do the same?

...

Tiet Linh and I work together as concert promoters, though each of us would deny being "partners" in any sense of that word. We do not share the profits from our mutual labours (there aren't any), though Tiet Linh often jokes that we share the liabilities of each other's company. That does not a "partnership" make, I say.

We've had our disagreements over the years as to the musicians we wanted to promote, and not only because of our own aesthetic preferences, but because such choices would bear on the composition of our audience—the very community we sought to create on these errant weekend nights. In the late 1980s we filled the stage of a community centre on Victoria Drive with old-fashioned *cai luong* singers—they were in easy supply, as

I recall, all those keening singers in high-necked silk *ao dai* dresses—and were thusly rewarded with a lukewarm assemblage of the curious, idle elderly. In the early 1990s I took the initiative of promoting New Wave acts, and we were able to fill the gyms of various East Vancouver elementary schools with Vietnamese covers of Krisma. Tiet Linh, however, thought we had gone too far with attracting a certain segment of the floppy-haired youth with their Glow Sticks and marijuana cigarillos, driving everyone else out into the moonlight. After much tussling back and forth between us, we have settled on a variety show format (perhaps reminiscent of the *Paris by Night* series) featuring a revolving tray of singers, but always with the Aquamarines as the backup band, these former South Vietnamese soldiers in hepcat berets and fedoras. This has worked well: you can now find all the generations at one of our concerts.

Whenever Anh Binh saw us arguing, he would smile with the masked equanimity of a dentist (he was, in fact, a dentist) and shake his head. Arguments over whether, for instance, the reds and yellows of the old South Vietnamese flag should always appear somewhere on the grandstand. Or whether, as master of ceremonies, I should stop wearing the same brown suit and bespoke tie (I believed my trademark attire was important for brand recognition, while Tiet Linh thought it begged more the mood of Sunday church). Although Anh Binh often played the mediator, to him our fights were at once absurdly quotidian and impracticably philosophical.

I knew that Anh Binh was dying when Tiet Linh and I stopped arguing—when she started nodding at whatever I said, looking for ghosts.

...

We were all young together in Hue, the old imperial capital in central Vietnam. All four of us had known each other in somewhat more innocent times, before that awful year of 1968 when Hue was held captive by the Communists for a month (how awful we thought that month was, but how little did we know what was ahead). I was living with my wife in my family's home, and Tiet Linh was living with Anh Binh in his. We were all in the same neighbourhood near the university, just south of the Perfume River, where Tiet Linh and I studied literature and art history respectively, and Anh Binh was studying to be a dentist.

My wife, meanwhile, was already making a living as a nurse and bone-setter (a trade passed on by her father to his only child). My wife's name was Ngoc, meaning "gem," and her mind was as sharp as one; she was a practical gem, a diamond not an emerald—not only beautiful but able to drill.

The Communists came during Tet, the Vietnamese New Year. The noise that in my memories could be heard above the firecrackers was the teeth of the old women chatter-chiming from door to door of our neighbourhood, like electricity running down a live wire, for it was the old women who felt the advance of the Viet Cong deep inside them—all those angry sons coming home to roost upon their mothers' ringing bones. The Communists were looking for people like Tiet Linh and me, the intellectuals and the Catholics. We escaped through the back while the soldiers knocked on our front doors.

We scrambled on foot down dusty roads with a flood of humanity that was equal parts panic and resignation, as the Communists took over the Citadel north of the Perfume River, and the south bank. The Communists had planted their flag high behind the stone walls of the Ngo Mon gate, and we made sure our backs were to it. We made it out of the city to a farmhouse in Anh Binh's ancestral village, all four of us crowding in with Anh Binh's aunts, uncles, grandparents, and assorted nephews and cousins.

During the month that it took the Americans and the South Vietnamese to retake Hue, both Anh Binh and Ngoc worked in the village hospital, where they tended to the civilian casualties that overflowed the hospital beds. Anh Binh even conducted rudimentary surgeries. A doctor was a doctor even if he was a dentist. It was no time for fine discernments.

Meanwhile Tiet Linh and I hid on the farm. During our first days we helped with the rice planting, though neither of us were trained to work on our haunches in the flooded paddies, and we both took turns falling headfirst into the mud, imprinting our bodies on the crushed stalks of newly transplanted seedlings. Mostly we read while waiting like children for our spouses to return from work. While we argued the finer points of Sartre or whether the French treated the Vietnamese worse than the Vietnamese treated its Cham minority, our spouses cut into bone and swept away entrails. They always came home late and too tired to talk, often with traces of blood on their clothes. How could two such soft-spoken and practical people be married to the likes of Tiet Linh and me? Anh Binh would retire with his wife to the main house, while Ngoc and I slept on the packed-dirt floor of the kitchen, where Ngoc would stare at the thatched roof in darkened amazement. She was a city girl and wondered where the chimney was for the cool metal stove that we rested our feet against.

"It's a thatched roof," I said. "The smoke rises right through it."

Even after what she must have seen each day at the hospital, Ngoc still had the energy to look at me wide-eyed with disbelief, but she did not argue. This discussion of porousness made me think of the Communist invasion, and I talked of how the Communists weren't bringing us a revolution but, like the French, were just trying to "civilize" us in their own terrifying ways. Ngoc replied with a purr of breath. She had left me for her dreamland and soon I fell asleep as well. Amazing how still those nights were, with that many people under one roof, the only noise the soft burps of distant shelling.

When we returned to Hue after the month-long siege, my home was one of the few in the neighbourhood still standing. Bicycles wobbled over tank tracks. Before entering the house, we paid our respects to the Spirit of the Soil as if we were building a new house. Everything inside the house was destroyed. Books and photos were ripped down the middle of the paper, as if by a petulant child. The wires of anything electric were torn out of their bellies. By these signs the Communists were telling us what they would have done if they had laid their hands on us. I followed Ngoc into our bedroom as if we were newlyweds — carefully following the tradition of not letting the bride step on the groom's shadow. It was only much later that we realized the extent of the civilian massacre during the occupation, that the hastily turned soil of the bare fields in Hue hid mass graves.

···

We were only days away from the New Year's concert and I was left to do everything. Tiet Linh and I used to have a clear division of labour: I was in charge of the venue and she took care of the musicians. I booked the high school gym or the community hall, rented the sound and strobe machines, called up Ba Kim for the *banh mi* sandwich catering, made sure enough glossy New Year's tickets were printed. Tiet Linh made sure that the musicians were happy. I preferred my job.

Now that they could not reach Tiet Linh, the artists started calling my cellphone at all hours of the day. One diva called me while I was on shift in my cab demanding to know why she was in the lineup right after another diva who sings in the same tea-gargling style. How should I know? Then there was Ong Chinh, the civil engineer-cum-balladeer who called me while I was at peace eating my bowl of *bun bo Hue* to remind me to bring some marbles, with which he plugs his ears so that he can better concentrate on stage. Why doesn't he just supply his own marbles? I tried to keep my composure, but then Johnny Nguyen called, his act our sole remaining homage to the New Wave. We have kept him on retainer though he has gone bald and continually defies our ban on Styrofoam cups.

"What do you want?" I said.

"Just saying *chao*, Bac Gia. How's it going?"

"How would I know? I'm on the stool."

"That's cool."

Tiet Linh *oi*, wherever you are, you must come out of your hiding.

...

All that Hue is for me now is the Forbidden Purple City, which lay in the very centre of the imperial fortresses of the Citadel. The Citadel itself is a massive walled city surrounded by a moat, and within it are the Palace of Supreme Harmony and other palaces and temples, the

Halls of the Mandarins, the imperial pleasure gardens. Commoners may have walked among such grandeur during the reign of the emperors and even after the American War, though much of it was by then in ruins. The Forbidden Purple City, however, was the emperor's personal residence, accessible only to his family and eunuchs. It was levelled in 1947, years before the first American soldiers set foot in the country. I have only ever seen photographs of the Forbidden Purple City — a single series of photographs, actually. And yet it is my most vivid image of Hue, the one that pushes out all my other memories.

I've been having the hardest time remembering the flamboyant tree that grew outside my home, the only one still standing on my block after the siege. I've tried to locate my quiet neighbourhood on Google Street View, but it has completely changed, and in its place are gleaming motorcycles parked beside bustling storefronts. Most of the videos on YouTube about Hue, though, are of the Citadel — perhaps because of all the nostalgia that the Citadel provokes. Or rather the sentimentality. I recently learned that the word *nostalgia* pertains to memory, and most people who use YouTube as a resource have no real memories related to the imperial palaces. If forgetting about the Forbidden Purple City meant that my other memories of Hue would be uncovered, then I would choose to forget about the Forbidden Purple City.

But then again, perhaps I am also guilty of "sentimentality," because the monuments of the Forbidden

Purple City had long burned down by the time I myself dwelled within the Citadel's walls, after the siege. I was only present at the Forbidden Purple City when it was bare ground marked by loose foundations.

During the siege, the Communists used its bare grounds as an operations base. Most of the surrounding palaces were also levelled by the siege's end. This was the state of the Citadel as I remember it best: the crushed bricks within the piles of timber, the scent of ancient ironwood columns split down their seams, releasing an oddly fresh smell of pine. This was the smell of my livelihood.

I managed to escape being drafted by the South Vietnamese army, and a couple of years after the siege I was employed as a historical consultant by the archaeological institute overseeing the conservation. No one, however, heeded my advice on proper restoration materials, and I was relegated to physical labour and being the site's de facto security guard. I spent most of my days, nights even, within the Citadel's brick walls. By this time the floating bodies had been pulled out of the moat and peasants were cultivating a water-borne spinach in the Royal Canal. I camped on these grounds as part of my restoration work, though *restoration* may not be the right word. The war was still on and resources were scarce. *Preservation* is perhaps a more suitable term, as it was not so much a matter of rebuilding as trying to clear the rubble into coherent piles throughout the palace grounds, *vo* bricks and tiles on one side, timber on another, mindful that some of the peasant volunteers were just there to steal ironwood to warm their hearths. I carried a French service pistol to wave at marauders. Meanwhile, Anh Binh volunteered on weekends to erect scaffolding to hold up the imperial roofs. He was paler than most of the labourers, having spent most of his days indoors, but he had a solid build and a greater stamina for hardship.

We did what we could. The levelled palaces did not rise again, but neither did the remaining ones fall, including the Palace of Supreme Harmony, where the emperor had greeted subjects on his throne. Everything changed once again in 1975, when the Communists took over for good. At first they wanted to destroy all the remaining palaces as symbols of imperialism, but Ho Chi Minh himself saved the Citadel, saying that because it was built on the backs of peasants, it belonged to the peasants. As a restorer, I was suddenly doing the People's work. My life was preserved. I had hope.

The Communists continued the work of restoring some of the monuments in the Citadel, and I was retained once again as a historical consultant until I fled the country in 1980. But all my advice to the authorities on maintaining authenticity went in one ear and out the other. This was before UNESCO became involved with their Western standards of original materials and ancient means; instead, the local authorities favoured jerry-rigged restoration methods using whatever was available.

I was a party to their sins. During my tenure at the Citadel I climbed dilapidated palaces to help roof them with crinkled metal. I sprayed ironwood columns with DDT to protect them from termites, making the wood's complexion ashen. Most of the original columns had actually been harvested by the marauders (I was helpless to stop them — they knew I wouldn't shoot), and I joined the other labourers in replacing the wooden beams with a type of ferroconcrete. On orders from my superiors, and with tears in my eyes, I held a quivering paintbrush over an antique pedestal, smothering whatever original gilt was left with an industrial paint.

Ngoc was always worried I would shoot my mouth off with a bourgeois remark at a cadre member and be hauled off to the re-education camps. The way the Communists were handling the project made me feel as if I was standing on uncertain ground to continue as a historical consultant, and this feeling manifested itself one morning in 1977 when, during a rooftop foot patrol, I tripped over a piece of jutting concrete. I broke my ankle. Ngoc, so busy at work, now had to set my bones for free while I lay on our bed biting on a rolled-up reed mat. She rubbed a paste made from her father's secret recipe over my heel and up my shin that dried into a cast, then secured my mess of a foot with bamboo splints and bandages. I had made it through the whole war without breaking a bone in my body; now I stayed in bed for several weeks — the worst time in my life. For my wife it was the best time, she said, because for once she knew exactly where I was.

Once my ankle healed and I was able to hobble under my own power, I returned to the Citadel. I still slept on the grounds of the Forbidden Purple City, but now it was only once a fortnight and largely for nostalgic reasons, for after my absence I realized how pointless my labours were. The remaining palaces around the Forbidden Purple City were more beautiful at night, when their perfect forms were backlit by the moon and one didn't notice the broken roof tiles of the emperor's writing pavilion or the bamboo scaffolding holding up the roof of the Palace of Supreme Harmony. At night the workmen's laundry hanging from the moon-shaped windows turned into horse-dragons.

One night I was standing in a minor pavilion overlooking a lotus pond and contemplating its eerie stillness when, through the beating horn-song of the cicadas, I heard the approach of footsteps. I was hobbling on a cane, no longer had my service pistol, and thought my ghost had come for me. And then I heard a familiar sniffling.

"What are you doing here?" I said.

It was Tiet Linh. She was carrying a lantern in her hands, royal yellow in colour and diamond-shaped. The size of a pineapple. She held it out towards me—a gift.

"I'm worried about you," she said. "Hobbling about in the dark. You're going to break your one good foot."

I didn't believe this was why she had come, of course, but I received her gift all the same. I put my lighter to the wick inside the lantern, and hung it off the lip of a carp-shaped rain sluice on the roof. I had not realized how dark the night was until that moment. Now I could see the flicker of the dragonflies just above the lily pads.

"You didn't come here just to give me a lamp, did you?"

"I came to see the restoration."

Again, I didn't believe her; why would she come at night? "Why are you interested?"

"History students don't have a monopoly over history," she said, referring to our ongoing quibble over which of our respective subjects was the superior undertaking.

"The Communists are building an approximation," I said. "Which is the same as a desecration." We looked out into the darkness towards the flag tower. The cicadas were getting louder, as if closing in.

"It's a desecration now," she said.

"No, it is in ruins now," I said. "That is something completely different." All the destruction around us was a result of war, which in Vietnam was a natural occurrence. What the Communists wanted to do was unnatural. To reclaim the past, they were willing to sweep away reality.

"Are they going to rebuild the Forbidden Purple City?"

"*Goi oi*, don't get me started," I said. I had heard rumours that one day, perhaps soon, they would start rebuilding in earnest, but one never knew what to believe from the Communists.

We went into the altar space of a pavilion and looked out into the flat grounds that had once been the Forbidden Purple City. It once consisted of over fifty

buildings culminating in the emperor's residential palace. Rice paddies took up a good part of the grounds
now. All that was left of the emperor's residential palace
were some floor tiles and a little stairway, a few forlorn
pedestals, a pair of brass cannons.

She was smiling wickedly at me. "Imagine what it must
have looked like," she said.

"I can't even begin," I said. There were no blueprints
left of it, no photos. I feared that the Communists were
just going to make something up out of thin air. Probably
just a copycat of the Beijing palaces.

"You can begin with this," said Tiet Linh. She pulled
something out of her handbag: another gift, a small
stack of old black-and-white postcards tied with a string,
worn along their edges. "I found this in my grandfather's
bedroom," she said. "It's from the 1920s."

I shuffled the postcards in my hands. Most of them
were the typical portraits of exotic *Indochine* that the
French colonials liked to send home — of water buffaloes
in rice fields, of turbaned subjects hovering over bowls
of strange food, or of naked courtesans holding opium
pipes. But among these old photographs were a few with
pristine edges, which crackled as I peeled them off, as
if new.

"Yes, look," she said. "They took pictures of the Forbidden Purple City before it burned down."

I held one postcard up and took my time flipping
through each photo, then looked back out to the rice
paddies. I could see it all clearly now: the flying eaves of

the grandest palace, the royal theatre and tea pavilion, the covered walkways where the eunuchs tiptoed towards their conspiracies.

The postcards were only of the exterior of the Forbidden Purple City; to this day no photos of the inside of the emperor's private residence are known to exist. And yet it is the insides that I saw most clearly in my mind. The sleeping chamber with its posh linens over smooth, hard beds. The kitchen with its artisans carving peacock garnishes out of carrots. Dragons and clouds painted on the columns in the various rooms. Poems in Chinese characters set in relief. These rooms have grown ever more vivid in my imagination each day since, with ever more perfectly authentic detail. My mind is so crowded now with such details of my own making that I sometimes hold my stomach in pain.

I handed the postcards back to Tiet Linh. Then, as quickly as her spirits lifted, her face cracked.

"Anh Binh is leaving me," she said. She was tearing up.

"Don't be silly."

"I don't trust him anymore," she said.

At the time I had no context for her statement, but the next year, in 1978, Anh Binh disappeared. Tiet Linh kept mum about his whereabouts, even let us believe he was dead, until we found out that he had re-emerged on the other side of the ocean, in Vancouver. He had escaped by boat under cover of night.

"You must have had a fight, that's all," I said. "You should go home. I'm sure Anh Binh is worried about you."

"He can wait," she said. She wanted me to show her the Citadel as I knew it.

We left the grounds of the Forbidden Purple City and walked towards the pleasure gardens. I took her to a little pontoon boat hidden in the corner of the lotus pond and I pretended to be the emperor and she one of my eunuchs. I paddled, we serenaded the moon, and Tiet Linh recited her favourite lines from *The Tale of Kieu*:

> *Due to my dismal generosity in past lives,*
> *I have to accept much suffering as compensation*
>   *in this life.*
> *My body has been violated as a broken pot,*
> *I have to sell my body to repay for my mournful fate.*

"How depressing," I said, though she sang the lines lightly, like a summer lullaby.

"Do you remember during the siege, when your wife and my husband would come home together, always tired and silent?"

"It was another life," I said.

"Didn't you ever wonder about them?"

"Not at all," I said. "Never." And I meant it.

...

I love *hope*, that is, the English word. My English sentence making is very good, though to this day my passengers sometimes have trouble understanding me because of my thick accent. I love the English language, though, how irreducible it is. *Hope* is true English, unlike *optimism*, which is an immigrant from the Latin world, with its messy notions of power and having the best. Such a pure word is *hope* that it cannot be broken down any further and stands for only itself—like those primal words meant to invoke animal sounds. *Meow. Ruff. Hope.* Even the Vietnamese term for hope, *hy vong*, isn't so pure. Taken apart, *vong* can mean "an absurdity."

An absurdity—that is *hope* in Vietnamese.

...

There was a knock on my door the night before the New Year's Day concert. I grabbed a Club, the elongated metal steering wheel lock, before answering. I keep a few extra Clubs around, for they are handy for more than securing the steering wheel of my cab. I rent a laneway house in East Vancouver about two cab lengths long, with tin-thin walls and my bedroom window hugging the property line by the back alleyway. One can never be too cautious.

It was the musician—the man—hugging one of his instrument cases, the one in the shape of a small coffin. The *dan bau*. The overhead lamp illuminated scratches on his face, a wicked play of shadows deepening the grooves, darkening his tears into blood drops.

"Bac Gia," he said, "I apologize for the disruption. But I was given your address, and I..."

"Your wife did this?" I knew the answer, but took some satisfaction when he nodded to confirm my insights into the artistic temperament.

"May we stay the night?" he said.

I let him in, though there was no room for both of us to sleep unless I moved my kitchen table outside, which I was loath to do. I surrendered my bed to him and after he took his shoes off he quickly fell asleep, his instrument by his side, as if he had always lived here. I tried to sleep in my cab, but soon gave up and turned on the ignition.

I drove to Tiet Linh's house. I parked in the back alley and jimmied the gate to the yard. I knew that it would be futile if I rang any of the doorbells—her daughter would surely answer the door and shoo me away—and so I reached down to the ground and gathered some pebbles. I took the back-porch stairs up to the second-floor landing, stopping at the sight of a black metal cauldron gleaming between the wooden steps. It was a new Broil King, untarnished by charcoal dust or oil splatters. Anh Binh must have bought it just before he died.

At the top of the landing I tossed the pebbles one at a time (the way I throw bread at the swans in Vancouver's Lost Lagoon) at Tiet Linh's bedroom window. Her pallor was ghostly as she drew back the blinds. In the moonlight haze she looked just as she had that night in the Forbidden Purple City.

"I didn't come here to serenade you," I said. "And I'm not here to offer you any pity."

"That's fine, as long as you're not looking for any from me."

"You can't just disappear."

"If it's about the musician, he has nowhere to go. You can send him to a hotel and bill me."

"I knew it was a bad idea to get these young people pretending to be old-time musicians," I said. "It's unnatural." I could tell that what I said enlivened her, because her cheeks darkened into what in the daylight would have been a bright vermilion.

"Unnatural! You always claimed to be a historian, but you never had an appreciation for the old crafts. You have no ear for traditional music."

"Oh! Oh!" I said. "Don't get me started!" But by now we couldn't stop ourselves from entering that dark debate about whether *vong co* music had any value. I argued against the music with more vehemence than I actually felt. Tiet Linh's daughter came to the window, only to be waved away by Tiet Linh, who was in mid-volley about some esoteric point. We were waking up the dogs in the neighbourhood, but we didn't care. It was quite some time before I walked back down the stairs to my cab. I took one last look at the Broil King.

"You can't just disappear!" I said again, but by now Tiet Linh's window was closed and all the lights were out.

...

Among the four of us, Tiet Linh and I were known as the dreamers and Anh Binh and Ngoc as the schemers. Anh Binh was the first one to escape Vietnam, and Tiet Linh followed him the next year. Anh Binh then came up with a plan to sponsor me to Canada as his brother, even though we were unrelated. We shared the same last name — Nguyen — and never mind that about half of Vietnam shared this surname: his scheme worked. I would just have to find a way to get to Vancouver.

When I told Ngoc to pack her things, she told me to go ahead without her. I was furious. She said she had a few things to tend to first with family and work, but that I shouldn't delay in going and that she would join me soon thereafter. I left by boat with an uneasy feeling in my stomach, one that didn't go away during the five months I spent at a refugee camp in Hong Kong, nor when I finally arrived in Vancouver. I had forgotten to bring a picture of Ngoc, not even a little wallet-sized photo. I thought it funny then. No matter, I thought, I would see her soon enough.

Ngoc passed away a year after I arrived in Vancouver. She was, in fact, ill before then, and knew of her prognosis in Vietnam when I asked her to leave with me. Just like Anh Binh, she was a practical schemer and she wanted to leave me with my dreams unscathed.

I still dream of the Forbidden Purple City. These days the Citadel is being restored with the expertise and funding of UNESCO and of countries as far-flung as Korea, Germany, and Poland. Now they use *vo* bricks and traditional tiles in the reconstruction. Ironwood has replaced the ferroconcrete, buffalo glue is now used, and the palaces are mortared by an authentic mixture of sugar cane molasses, lime, and local sand. I've been watching the progress on YouTube, the Forbidden Purple City rising in its vivid red splendour among the original palaces of the Citadel that remain, the colours of their tiles and columns dull by comparison. For a small price tourists can dress like the emperor and take photos in the palaces with a consort of actors playing eunuchs. With all the chaotic occurrences on YouTube, I can't tell sometimes what is a documentary of the reconstruction and what is a historical melodrama. But altogether it is as though the war never happened. It is as though there was never any reason for us to leave the country.

...

When I arrived home from Tiet Linh's house, the *dan bau* player was gone. My first thought was to call the police, but he had taken nothing from me. Then I worried about his own safety, but there was nothing I could do. Tiet Linh would not answer my texts or my phone messages.

The next evening I walked to the site of the New Year's concert, a high school gymnasium not too far from where I live. As is my routine, I arrived a couple of hours before the start. I carried an uneasy feeling in my belly at the chaos that would reign in Tiet Linh's absence. To my great relief, though, the ticket-punch girl was already there, resplendent in her *ao dai* and setting up her table at the entrance. Inside the gym, Ba Kim rolled in her *banh mi* sandwiches on trays and my trusted volunteers were tying colourful streamers. Someone had already placed a small *hoa mai* tree on the stage and hung red ribbons off its yellow-blossomed branches. Men from the light and strobe company were moving cables across the polished gym floor and put before me a clipboard with a voucher to sign. I should have known, of course, that the world would go on without the likes of Tiet Linh and me.

Soon the Aquamarines arrived and started unpacking their drum kits and guitars. Then I heard a commotion in the back dressing room and put my hands over my stomach: the divas had already arrived. I walked to their room, their voices echoing off the plastered brick wall of the hallway — the *cai luong* singers, the engineer-cum-balladeer, the aging New Waver. And then I heard one more voice among them, a very welcome one. Tiet Linh's. I stepped inside.

"We were wondering about you," she said. They were all laughing and Tiet Linh's eyes were puffy. They had been talking about Anh Binh. By now Tiet Linh had already arbitrated the lineup and taken care of all the musicians' personal needs — marbles for the engineer, Styrofoam cups for the New Waver.

"Where are the *vong co* musicians?" I asked.

Tiet Linh had no answer. "He came back to my house last night," said Tiet Linh, "and then the two left together. Who knows if they'll show up?"

"The artistic temperament knows no boundaries," I said.

"At least of decorum," she said.

I left Tiet Linh to her musicians and tended to the details of the stage. There were too many problems to deal with in the time remaining, but when the rafter lights were lowered and the strobe lights came on, I could no longer see any imperfection. The crowd filtered in and took their seats at the long cafeteria tables, and I took my customary seat off to the side. All the generations came, from grandparents my age in suits and ties or *ao dai*s and evening pearls to young people who wore as much mascara and glitter on their clothes as the performers did. The old danced the cha-cha to the standards while the young sang along to new numbers.

The evening flowed as harmoniously as any other until midway through the concert when the rafter lights came back on. The Aquamarines then left the stage except for the guitarist, who replaced his instrument with a moon lute. The rafter lights dimmed again and the spotlight froze on a couple resplendent in ancient dress. Our *vong co* players had come after all.

The man stood behind his *dan bau*, its single string untouched yet already resounding, its buffalo-horn spout rising from its gourd, its lacquered soundboard shimmering in the strobe light. The woman turned to her husband and appeared to smile before stepping up to the microphone.

Tiet Linh joined me at the table, looking eternal in her own *ao dai*. The crowd cheered as soon as the first notes of "Da Co Hoai Lang" were released from the moon lute. This was the song that gave birth to the genre—written by Cao Van Lau, who was forced by his mother to dispense with his wife after three years of a barren marriage. A legend persists that the poor composer would choke up every day he brought home his catch of crustaceans, because his wife was no longer present to sort the shrimps from the crabs. Old men wiped away tears when the singer chimed in above the moon lute. For much of the song her husband stood still and considered his *dan bau* with a silent stroke of his finger against the spout. When finally he struck his first note against the single string, his wife did not crack or hurl herself off the stage as I had feared. Rather she sang alongside the *dan bau*, whose note stood up as its own voice against hers, into a true duet of mourning.

The lights stayed low when the song finished, and a small girl came to the front of the stage to give pink flowers to both the wife and the husband. I looked over at Tiet Linh and her lips were crisply sealed with a look of endurance. How far we have made it, she seemed to say. I thought about how I had not had a chance to properly comfort her in the months since her husband and my good friend had passed away. I wanted to tell her that she didn't have to be alone. I wanted to say what I would have wanted to hear when my own wife passed away. I opened my mouth, but no words came, just a trembling of my lips.

"You don't have to say anything," said Tiet Linh.

I knew this was an act of kindness on her part.

I thought of our lives together, both on this and the other shore. I looked down at the table. "I can't see Ngoc's face anymore," I said. "I've tried everything, but I can't find her in my memory. It's been so long now."

Tiet Linh held my hand, to still it. Then she touched my chin and tilted it up towards the stage as the next singer took the microphone, as the drummer lifted his drumsticks.

Mayfly

You were twelve when you found your homies, but you didn't know this at first. You were starting grade seven at a new elementary school in that part of East Van where all the street names are Scottish like yours—Dumfries and Fleming and Killarney (years later you learned that Killarney was in fact Irish) — and your new school was named after some inventor of worldwide standard time. He could have been your ancestor, if your ancestors weren't instead boxcar hoboes who fled the Prairies during the Depression to sleep out on these west coast streets.

The year before, your mother, a corporate secretary at an insurance agency, got sick of your father and shacked up with her boss. She gave your father the heave and you moved out along with his few chattels to your grandfather's house, to be solid with your men-kin and because you couldn't stand your mother's boss-boo.

At your old school you would have been respected as one of the elder peckers, but here you had built up no goodwill, hadn't yet hit puberty, and your face was as pale as milk, splattered with punch-me freckles. You soon attracted the bullies. They stole your turkey sandwiches during the lunch recess. On a rainy day, when you sought shelter under the covered hopscotch walk, they chased you out because they used the walk for their ball hockey games. Then they took your nylon poncho for their goalie to wear inverted like a straitjacket, to trap the tennis ball-puck.

You were left in the rain-drenched playground among second- and third-graders who were digging trenches into the muddy ground around the wooden see-saws and rusted tire swings. You went to another side of the school to find a dry awning. And that's where you found them. Huddled and looking as cold as you out in the rain, though they were wearing sweaters and nylon jackets.

They spoke in a strange language. The youngest was your age, but most were older. One had a moustache. Some were smoking. Others sucked juice boxes. Some pointed fingers at you, and you didn't know whether they were talking to you or to each other. Then the Moustache took off his sweater jacket and tossed it at you, and you ducked. Then one of them stepped behind you. You were surrounded. You put up your fists, elbows at right angles like a boxing leprechaun. And then they grabbed your waist from behind and you couldn't move, and then they pulled your shirt over your head and spun you around, and you couldn't see again until your shirt was pulled right off. Now you were bare-chested with steam rising off your pricked nipples. And then the Moustache picked up his sweater jacket from the pavement and handed it to you. "Put it on," he said. Dry wool calmed your cold, wet skin.

He had your shirt and rolled it up into a rope, then squeezed all the rainwater out. Then the youngest one held a blue Thermos in front of your face and unscrewed the plastic cap. As you leaned into the Thermos, into the glowing aluminum inner canister, steam from a beefy broth crawled up your cheeks. He poured the soup into the upturned cap and you sipped. Your belly warmed and you could feel your toes again.

The next time you checked the awning, they were gone, though you felt their invisible presence like guardian angels. This made you brave, and though you did not pick fights, in the future you did not shy away from them. The next time someone tried to steal your poncho, you hit back. For that you got a black eye that would forever see floaters against the blue sky.

Later in winter, during another rainy recess, they were back under the awning. "You're skinnier," said the Moustache in his heavy accent. The others threw their cigarettes into a rutted puddle. Then the one around your age asked if you were hungry, and you nodded because you couldn't lie to him. "Come on then." His name was Sang.

You followed him to the grocery store, but before you went in, he asked if you had any money. You told him that you didn't, and he said he didn't either. "That's okay. Just be careful." You made it past the potted flowers under tarp at the front of the store, then inside to the aisles of dried goods. Sang disappeared down an aisle, leaving you staring at the Campbell's Soup labels. Then you heard the exit chime and went outside. Sang was running, and you followed his heels around a corner alley. He handed you his stash of bubble gum and Snickers. "On me," he said. "Next time, on you."

You didn't know when that next time would come. The homies disappeared into the shadows of your memory. Sometimes you thought you saw Sang in school, the black pricks of his buzz cut darting from fountain to classroom. You could never be too sure.

The next time, in spring, the bullies came for you in a pack, surrounded you by the basketball courts like this time they meant to make no mistake. Now you would be the turkey in their sandwich. They pinned you against the fence, but just when you were going to be devoured, in flashed that familiar prick of hair. Sang shoved one of them aside and freed your arms. Newly cocky, you took a punch at a bully. You thought Sang knew kung fu. You would have just run away if you had known the truth—that Sang had only come to offer his body in the beating, to spot his face for yours.

And so you both got your asses kicked. One of the boys dragged Sang by the legs and laid him out flat on the gravel, holding down his shoulders. Then the rest piled on top. You were enough of a pest, biting and kicking at shins, so that you and Sang managed to escape through the back alleys of the neighbourhood, past the shadows of blackberry bushes and cherry trees, the camouflage of barking dogs.

You had a gashed cheek, a fat lip, and only a mirror knew what else. You could not go home looking like you did. Or maybe you could. Maybe your grandfather would be proud and your father newly respectful of the scars that spoke of your bourgeoning manhood. But instead of going home, you followed Sang through the backyard of his house. His mother was waiting with angry resignation. She pulled an ostrich feather duster from a large urn at the entrance to their basement suite and swatted Sang with it. For a while mother and son went pug-nose to pug-nose. She did not look at you. After these soft lashings, Sang led you to the living room, and you were enveloped by a pungent air belonging to another latitude, thick with animal fat and incense.

When you returned to your grandfather's house, it was dark, and you felt your way around by the smells — the sourdough bread marking the kitchen, the polished cedar of his den where he was snoring, down into the basement past the rusted metal and motor oil of his workshop to the mildew in the bathroom.

Your grandfather had been a high rigger lumberjack. During World War II he took off the tops of spruce trees over twenty storeys high, up in the Interior, while his friends went off to face the Germans. You could not imagine any soldier matching your grandfather's blow-by-blow tales in the forests, and you learned from him that no tree was just a tree. You either felled it or it felled you.

You went to sleep not sure where your father was. He was a ghost who carried not much more about him than the smell of fabric softener and twitch of static. He was an electrician on disability, felled by something invisible. His war would have been Vietnam, if he had fought, though not having fought didn't stop him from cursing draft dodgers who made homes in his neighbourhood.

The next morning, your grandfather, as usual, slathered his sourdough bread with liverwurst, while your father buried his nose in cornflakes and a fishing magazine. Neither of them remarked upon your absence the night before or your re-emergence in battle-won glory.

A month later, Sang said next time on you was now, and you said you had no money, and he headed for the grocery store anyway, and you followed him. There the owner put you in a half nelson after you tried to pocket one of the wine gums and Fun Dip candies. You watched Sang walk right past you like you were a sorry stranger. The police came, but because you still hadn't hit puberty all you got was a kick-ass ride in a cop car right to your grandfather's front step. At least this time you got a rise out of your old man, and though his disability prevented him from beating you, he was able to clamp your fingers to open splices, submitting you to a low-level shock as your punishment for the day.

You didn't hit your spurt until the summer before high school, when your voice broke up, your lungs filled out, and your legs inched towards manhood. Lean and lanky, you were destined to become a baller. At the high school you took up junior varsity basketball. But you soon got tired of institutional ball, and preferred to be in civvies out on the asphalt in the open air, where there were hoops beside hopscotch charts or on the edges of tennis courts. After school you started looking for pickup games.

That was when you ran into the other homies again — on sunny days out on the cracked grey-tops. They were in Adidas hoodies and rolled-up sleeves. Some played in sneakers with no ankle support, and the Moustache was even in sandals.

Now with you they had numbers to play pure form, three-on-three. You, Sang, and the Moustache against the rest of the world. You hit nothing but net with your first shot, if only the bent rim had had a net. Sang, forever short, was the playmaking point, tossing the ball to you to swoosh all day with your jumper while the Moustache drove the basket with a Du Maurier between his lips.

You realized your worth when you played outsiders. Mostly Hongers and Namers at first, who you overpowered with quickness and height. Then the Sikhs came, and the game opened up to full-court five-on-five, with subs. The first time, you rained on them with your jumper, and when you drove the hoop, your homies cleared the lanes for you like cockroaches splashed with light. You thought you were unstoppable.

But that quickly changed. The Sikhs had matching forces. They had height to match yours. They swatted your jumpers. And when you were on defence they squeezed you in picks tight enough to pop your zits. Against the Sikhs, the Moustache couldn't keep a cigarette steady in his mouth and tore a strap off his sandal. Sang got his neck stuck in one of their armpits.

You played all night against the Sikhs and lost all your skins. When you got home your father gave you hell, but you didn't bother looking at him because he was just a gimp. You told him that on nights it didn't rain, he shouldn't be waiting up for you.

You were hanging with the homies on the weekends now all through grade eight, looking farther afield for games — up as far north as Strathcona, as far east as Burnaby. You would ride in their cars, most of the time in the Moustache's split-pea-yellow Datsun, a hatchback with all nose and no ass, and you had to squeeze in the back with three other homies. Others had sweeter rides, like a Mazda RX and a Toyota Supra with a souped-up spoiler.

Sometimes, if you had a hot night with your jumper, they would let you ride shotgun in the RX or the Supra. You could barely hear the engine purr in these cars, compared with the Moustache's Datsun. This cool hush, with the windows up and the streets rolling by, you would forever associate with the sound of money. You thought these rides were the cream Royale, because you were too hick to tell rice rockets from Ferraris and Porsches.

Your mother worried you were losing weight. You saw her once a week at the old house, which smelled of her perfumes and of the flowers that she would pick from front yards on her walk home from the bus stop, and that she would dry between the pages of her mystery novels. Sometimes you would have to endure the company of her boss-boo, who patted your head like a dog, and all you wanted was to bite his wrist off. Sometimes he would take you and your mother out for gelatos and asked if you ever thought of entering the insurance business. "All the time," you said.

Your mother used to dress poor but with class. Simple and clean lines, the same blouses ironed to perfection, a dab of Chanel behind each ear. Now she wore wind chimes on her ears, heels with more length than her skirts, and fishnet stockings to cover the distance. She had grown out her hair, permed it, teased it, and dyed it electric blonde.

Once she asked if your father was feeding you right. You nodded, but she made you lift your shirt to see your ribs. She gave you a hundred-dollar bill. "Eat right," she said. You took that bill to your homies and fronted all of them at the next skins game. Having your money on the line lit your ass aflame. Your jumpshots were keener. You stayed on your man through the tightest picks. This time you took the Sikhs down.

The Sikhs handed your homies a fat stack, but you never saw the take. Instead, the homies took you out for a sit-down meal at one of the neighbourhood pho joints.

It was a feast of God's creatures on land, sea, and air, on beds of rice and vermicelli noodles, drowned in fish sauce and tiny red peppers that made you want to cut your tongue off. The pretty waitresses passed around Coronas and you got high on your first bottle ever, the scars on your arms red from beer blush. The Moustache started a song, more like a chant, which caught on like a candle bent to a candle, and though you could not understand the words, you could slap the table at the same rousing rhythm as your homies. You had never been so high. The next time you saw your mother, you told her that yeah, you did eat right.

One day, in the undying light of summer after eighth grade, the Moustache threw you his keys and said you were driving. You had never turned a wheel and were still more than two years away from being licence eligible. "Just down the street," he said. "Easiest part of your day."

He was right. Even though you were just going thirty clicks down a little Scottish-named street, you felt like you were flying. And this was how you learned to drive — in the tight alleys and double-parked streets of East Van, where there was nowhere to go but slow and straight. You were scared a cop would pull you over driving without a pass, but the homies told you not to sweat it. "You are invisible to them," they said.

Now, in ninth grade, the Moustache threw you his keys every time you met him parked outside your school. They were right, the cops just drifted by so long as you could work the Datsun's stick. And pretty soon you weren't just driving straight lines from the school to the asphalt courts, but running errands. Pretty soon the Moustache wasn't waiting for you at the parking lot after school but told you to meet him at some side street, a different one each time. Then he'd come and pick you up with Sang in the back seat of a strange, beat-up car. He'd throw you the keys, take shotgun, tell you to drive straight or make a turn, but would not say where you were going. You'd only know the destination when he told you to brake at some alleyway between two backyards. Then the Moustache and Sang took off down the alley while you sat in the car listening to the woodpeckers in the fruit trees, paying no mind to the neighbours who returned the favour and paid no mind to you. The Moustache and Sang would come back panting and load up the trunk, sometimes with electronics — TVs, VCRs, video game consoles — sometimes with canvas bags holding what you couldn't tell. Then they told you to drive again — straight, left, right — to some strange corner, and then the Moustache would take back the keys and hand you some bus fare. The next time it was a different beat-up car. And then later you didn't just get a bus ticket, but a fanning slice of fives and tens. "Candy cash," said the Moustache. "Lollipop dough."

It went down like this for every errand you ran, and you hid your growing stash at home in a Danish cookie tin. That's where the money stayed, because you couldn't imagine what you wanted to blow your wad on.

One day in tenth grade the Moustache picked you up

right at the doorstep of your school, in another homie's Supra. He had it newly waxed so you could see your teeth in its black coat. He wasn't wearing his usual sorry tight jeans and scuffed sandals, but was in orange pants and black shirt buttoned to the collar with a sheen that matched the Supra's paint job. He coasted down the Knight Street Bridge south to Richmond, then through dirt roads running along steep ditches on both sides, past the cranberry and blueberry fields of the Agricultural Land Reserve, which was for you the heart of darkness.

The Moustache slowed at a chicken-wire fence with plastic slats that concealed what lay behind, and an electronic gate opened at the sound of his cawing. You also heard a rooster, which surprised you because in cartoons they only crowed at sunrise. A winding paved driveway cut through verdant pastures to a freshly baked McMansion, with Doric columns and Pop-Tart stucco siding. A squadron of rice rockets were parked on the grass beside a red wooden barn, and the Supra joined them.

You followed the Moustache, stepping over glistening barbells left on the grass, then past a set of tires laid side by side like an obstacle course. Free-range hens scurried past you, which the Moustache said weren't sold for money but instead kept for good fortune — not the same thing. He led you down the side of the McMansion, past the swivel glare of a CCTV camera, to the backyard the size of your neighbourhood park. All the homies were there, dressed up in celebration pastels. You could tell they were all in second-hands, with their pants a little too long or short, their done-up collars too tight or loose. Some wore varsity cardigans and ties with a fish-oil sheen loose around their necks. You felt analog and grainy in your torn jeans and scruffy T-shirt.

Not only were brothers in attendance but sisters as well. Two in bespoke skirts were clearing a long picnic table sloppy with metal parts you weren't then familiar with — recoil springs and hammer pins laid bare like gizzards. The sisters put a cloth over the table and then set out paper plates. The scent of fish sauce and grilled meat mingled with that of fresh-cut grass and some sort of machine oil, and all of it made you sick-hungry.

The sisters eyed you like they just bit on a lemon, and the Moustache told them it was okay, you were his boy now.

"Isn't that up to Brother Number 1?" they said.

The Moustache made the call to dinner, and you and your homies ate chastely at one end of the table, maybe because of the presence of the sisters eating at the other end. Sitting in the centre was a girl your age in a shimmering *ao dai* dress pinned with a corsage, her hair in an updo, and next to her was your boy Sang. This girl didn't touch her food or speak to anyone, but looked up around her shoulders every so often like she had lost a dragonfly, while Sang smiled like he won the 6/49 by getting to pour her tea, his hand on the back of her chair.

This was how it went down — guys on one end, girls on the other — and you ate with your brothers in silent communion like this had always been so, until sunset, when some pineapple-shaped lanterns that had been strung on chicken wire were lit up. Then someone turned on the ghetto blaster. The sisters knocked off their slippers and danced to "Poison" by Bell Biv DeVoe. Then the mix took on a west coast edge with Tupac and Ice Cube and Snoop Dogg, heating the waters just enough for the brothers to slide right in. Even the Moustache started kicking it. You stood up too, but drifted off to where the shadows of the apple trees grew long. Then, when Boyz II Men slowed things down, and hips on the dance floor stirred the Boyz' soft crooning with the milk-light from the night sky, and the brothers were sweet-talking the sisters in ways you didn't understand, all you could pay mind to was the girl in the corsage sitting by herself at the empty picnic table. The lantern shadows had carved a scowl across her cheek. Even Sang had left her side and put an arm around your neck.

"Fun?" he said.

"Mad fun," you said.

In the days after, when you were back at school or running errands with Sang, it was like that whole night was just in your head. You had to ask what went down with all that.

"Brother Number 1's birthday party," said Sang. "Or was supposed to be."

"The one who owns the joint?" you said. "I never saw him."

"His daughter wanted it to be a surprise, but he didn't show."

"You mean the girl in the corsage?"

"Corsage?"

"Yeah, your girl at the table," you said. "Your girl," you said again, which made Sang's teeth break out.

"Yeah, sure, my girl."

...

You got your licence the next year. Now you could mule around good and proper. One day you skipped school as usual to drive Sang and the Moustache to one alley or another. You got in the driver's seat, like always, and the Moustache took shotgun, but now there was another homie in the back, a sister that you could not place at first but whose eyes and pretty scowl rang a little gong. It was the scowl that brought you home again to that farm in Richmond. It was Brother Number 1's daughter, except now she had filled out in all the woozy-making ways. She was curvy for a sister, and her long legs stilettoed from jean shorts across the back seat of the Datsun, in bare feet, and she wore a tight yellow Canucks shirt with the waffle crest ready to explode, leaving a bare midriff with a waistline that perfectly framed her navel. You didn't even notice Sang in the corner, his Cheshire grin floating somewhere behind the girl's bent kneecaps. She was reading some sort of textbook, head resting against the corner-pocket windows, those legs again now stretching over Sang's lap.

"I don't think we've met," you said. Before you could offer your hand in respect, she gave you a once-over that kept it on the steering wheel.

"Just drive," she said.

You did as you were told, then braked at an alley off Dumfries Street. The two got out and the girl stayed put, and from the way it was going down you knew better than to say a word. You stole snatches of her through the rear-view while she read her textbook, something about sociology or biology or some other -ology. The clock melted slowly and you started wondering if your brothers had pawned the sister off onto you. But when Sang and the Moustache came panting back with their canvas bags and you booked it right-left-right to the final drop, and your boys saw you off with fist bumps, bus fare, and another nice slice, you thought all was good and calm again.

The next time was just back to you three. The Moustache joked about how you all should get extra for babysitting Brother Number 1's daughter, and hoped that you would not be called to such duty again.

But you were called again. She became part of the Routine, popping up in the back seat with some textbook and the scent of strawberries and rosewater. With her around, the Moustache kept his cigs in his pants and saved his patriotic anthems for the shower, while Sang sat in the back with his ass on his hands and grinning like no tomorrow.

Her English was better than yours, though she still

had a trace of that accent no amount of time could wash away. Her name was My Linh.

"You think you're babysitting me," she told you once when you were alone in the car with her. "You're wrong. I'm babysitting you."

"Like on orders from Brother Number 1?" you said. She looked like you had cracked a bad joke.

"That's what they call him. That's not what I call him."

"What do you call him?"

"Father when I need him. Nothing when I don't."

By next year you got tired of just being a driver, a babysitter, a mule. You gave the Moustache word that you wanted in on your homies' core competencies. He said he would run it by Brother Number 1, and though the great man had never even seen your face, you knew your wish was granted when the Moustache handed you a sub sandwich with both hands like it was on a velvet pillow. At home, you bit in and spat out a Post-it Note that was wedged between two slices of *cha lua* ham.

It was a shopping list: tuct tape, bottles of fertilizer and pesticides by the litre, rolls of extension cords, PVC piping, black plastic pots, bags of soil. You went to the Canadian Tire for the materials in a Buffalo Bill minivan on loan, and dropped off the goods with the Moustache.

"What are we doing, planting a garden?" you said. "Do you need me for this?"

"You're a Footman now," said the Moustache, "and maybe someday you'll be a Face."

But all you did was run more pickups at the Canadian

Tire. They still made you the mule. So next time you didn't bother heeding the Moustache's sub-sandwich call; you just stayed in your room, plugging out the sound of rain drooling down the drainpipes with your foam-puffed headphones. You didn't notice the tap-slap against the windowpane, at least not until it was jimmied opened and you felt the raindrops against the back of your neck, like someone was licking you softly.

You looked up. It was My Linh, in a nylon windbreaker.

Her cheeks were red and puffy and streaked with rainwater or tears, you couldn't tell. You didn't ask her how she knew to get to your crib. She would tell you what she wanted you to know, no more, no less.

She took off her kicks, pulled down her hoodie, and beneath it her hair was slick and black like eels. She dried off with some paper towels. Then she shoved your Dead Kennedys tapes off the E.T. blanket and sat with her back against the rodeo wallpaper, her knees propped up against her chest. She put on your headphones and listened to a couple of tracks from your DK mix, classics like "Holiday in Cambodia" and "Kill the Poor," then took the headphones off, looking like a tourist who had already seen this view. "Who's he?" she said, pointing at the opposite wall.

"John Stockton," you said. "Utah Jazz. Greatest point guard ever." With anyone else you would have called them on their ignorance. With My Linh, you pointed out that Stockton was not as flashy as a dunker but he was a deeper watch.

"So John Stockton was a Footman and not a Face," she said. "Is that what you want?"

Before you could answer, there was a knock, then your father opened the door. You sat completely still, as if you and My Linh would then turn invisible. He gave the girl a look over, said "Hello," then gently closed the door.

"What does he do?" she asked. You couldn't think fast enough to lie, but when you told her he was an electrician, her eyelashes flipped a switch. "You must know something about it too?"

You nodded, because as a kid you sometimes tagged along on one of his jobs, and whatever magic she saw in your dad you wanted a piece of it too.

Then you showed her the cookie tins under your bed, as if you needed her permission to keep them. She opened a lid and fingered the fat stacks, asked what you were going to do with them all. "Buy a Maserati," you said, though you had never had that urge before this very moment.

"You'll need more tins," she said.

You heard a shuffling at the door. Left on the carpet outside were a plate of cookies and two glasses of milk. My Linh swished the milk, skipped the cookies, then disappeared back out into the rain.

The next morning at the breakfast table your father looked up from his fishing magazine and smiled at you like you had been long lost and finally found.

"It wasn't like that," you said. "It's not like that at all."

A few days later the Moustache gave you another

gardening list. When you went to fetch the Buffalo Bill van, My Linh was waiting shotgun. You weren't expecting her, and would have combed down your red hair instead of just putting a cap on. You rode to the Canadian Tire like newlyweds laying out your first crib, picking up some halide bulbs and steel cables before scoring the rest of the list at other hardware stores so as not to attract notice. Then she told you the straight-left-rights to your final destination. It was Sang's house, except that the basement was bare now. Sang was standing in the backyard expecting you, though he didn't make eye when you offered a fist bump. He was still a baby-faced shorty but now was thick in the arms and neck, and gelled his brush cut back to cover a little bald spot where he had once been scalped. The gel made him smell like an open bucket of gasoline.

You and Sang unloaded the day's booty—the lengths of electrical coil and transformers, the vats of chemical fertilizer, the rolled-up sheets of poly. Each item in itself was innocuous, but the composite of your intent was clear. You worked in broad daylight because, according to My Linh, that way you wouldn't be noticed. At night, if you made any noise or had the lights on, you'd be seen and known.

My Linh shooed Sang upstairs so that she and you could concentrate. In the basement, you stood beneath her as she went up a stepladder to cut a hole in the ceiling. You brushed plaster dust off your face then handed her the vent tubing, which she snaked through the hole.

She got you to hang the zip lines and then the overhead lights. Then you watched her staple the poly sheets against the edge of the ceiling, how she arched her back like the Peking Circus to hammer the stapler above her head.

When she finished, she showed you where the concrete floor was cut to bypass the electrical meter. "That's your job," she said. She got you to move the transformers to a wooden shelf, then opened the electrical panel and waved her wrist like a game show hostess in front of the bus bars. "Work your magic," she said. Your job was to divert power from its natural course, away from the stove, dryer, and refrigerator, to feed the lights that would feed the plants. Your magic trick was to turn Sang's basement into a tropical hothouse.

"The homies who did this before fried themselves and one of our houses," she said. "I have never seen my father so pissed."

You took one of the wires and drew it over one of the bus bars. My Linh stood behind you and watched. You didn't know how to make the right connections. All you could see was the tip of your nose, all you could hear was your own hard breathing. You didn't know if you had the right wires spec'd to do the job, but the wrong ones could get you fried, that much you knew. Your hand froze over the bus bar, unable to make contact.

My Linh took your hand in hers, then the wire. "I'll do it," she said.

You watched over her shoulder while she took out the breakers from the panel board, connected the white and yellow wires together into a funky spiderweb. You could feel the static from the hum of her fingers over the bus bars, the blood charging red in your face.

"You've done this before," you said, and she told you to hush.

"Just watch," she said. She flipped a switch and you heard a sizzle. All the appliances had been killed and you and she were now standing under the intense glow of the grow lights. Her smiling face shone white like an eggshell, and you felt like you were the chick beneath the heat lamp, ready to crack out.

"Now all we need for a grow op are the plants," you said.

She put a finger to her lips. "Don't even say the word," she said. "You don't see any plants. You just set up the houses."

Sang came down with two plates of fried rice, one for My Linh and one for himself. "Gotta earn your keep," he said.

"Take mine," said My Linh, and handed you her plate and shared Sang's plate and spoon. "Next time he will," she told Sang.

You and she became an item, sort of, wiring up basements in East Van and shacks in Richmond at-grade. You learned the wiring from her and she had learned it from Brother Number 1 himself, tagging along as a child when he started this racket because her mom had passed on and her father had no daycare. She said she'd look over your shoulder until you got a handle on things.

It had been years since you went balling with your

homies or even did their muling. Now you only saw them when you were wiring up a house, like when Sang and the Moustache would come in the basement and dump their day's loot, the hot jewels or electronics, like it was show-and-tell for My Linh to see. They talked around you in their own language and snickered glances your way.

Sometimes they came in with pots of the fully grown weed, lining the empty basement with trembling ferns and that musky smell. My Linh told you they were grow-rips from rivals. "Not like we need them," she said, "but more to teach the poseurs a lesson. So they know not to dare to compete."

Soon you were wiring up grows with a skill that might have made your father proud. But you wanted to be a looter, and so you got the Moustache to let you tag along with him and Sang during their midday raids, with another shorty who was muling by the wheel.

They made it look easy. The Moustache had spent weeks casing the crib in advance and knew when the cats inside would leave it empty, usually in the middle of the school day. The Moustache knew which window needed to be jimmied or whether you could walk right through a sliding door.

Your on-court panther skills served you well as a looter. You displayed superior patience, and while Sang's head did three-sixties from the buzz of panic, you took your sweet time poking under all the nooks and crannies. Even the Moustache got nervous waiting for you, flicking a phantom cigarette, though you always came through with a little something extra if they just kept faith. You had a knack for sniffing out hidden jewels and bills stashed by the beaten-down wife under a loose square of carpet or behind a hockey trophy.

Once, Sang was so done waiting he locked himself in a bathroom to piss out all the Vietnamese iced coffees he had chugged at lunch. The bathroom had an old-school hook-and-eye latch that was so rusted Sang couldn't unhook the eye when the owners' car started raking the gravel driveway. You managed to dart back to the alley, not knowing that Sang was still inside tugging on the door and softly wailing. The Moustache had to kick the door down and pull Sang out with his fly unzipped and piss down his pants. Afterwards, safe in your ride, Sang gave you no fist bump.

Stealing pearls and stereos from unsuspecting civilians was easy. An enemy's grow op, though, was a different game, one you weren't yet allowed to play. You heard about their fortifications from the homies who made it back from a grow-rip, sometimes with their blood trailing on the carpet. There were pit bulls to be wary of, both animal and human. There were coyote traps set at the basement entrance, or venomous darts set off by a tripwire hidden within electrical cables, or sometimes just a silent alarm tripped by a CCTV camera calling forth silent assassins from south of the Fraser River.

The homies on grow-rip detail were the stealthiest of Brother Number 1's henchmen, all of them slick and bird-boned, with slitted eyes that seemed to let in no light and betrayed no longing. They were the ones who drove the Ferraris and Maseratis.

You wanted in. You had now reached the age of majority and had had enough of these mom-and-pop loots. You were stuck venting another basement while My Linh was laying out the cords and the Moustache was emptying his pockets from yet another raid. When you uttered your wish, My Linh kicked the ladder from under you and you pulled the venting down with your fall.

"Dumb-ass," she said. "You so don't know what you're getting into."

"I know there's fat stacks in it," you said.

The Moustache said that Sang wanted in on grow-rips too, and that you could go together.

"You need to talk to my father first," said My Linh.

My Linh pencilled you in for a meeting at HQ in the next quarter. In the meantime you got a pointillist tattoo by some scratcher on Main Street, of the Canadian flag entwined with the red banner and yellow star of Vietnam. When you showed your left shoulder off to My Linh, she snarled, took a swipe, and left claw marks on the fresh dotwork.

"Fool with the Communist signal," she said. "You got your victors and vanquished all mixed up. And have you ever seen any other homie with a tattoo? Keep your skin clean. That's my father's first rule."

You put a finger to your shoulder, smiled at your blood that she left as her mark. "What's the second rule?" you asked.

"Keep your thoughts pure," she said.

On the appointed day the Moustache picked you up in his beater. You were heading to Brother Number 1's farm in Richmond. It was harvest season. Sang did the muling, the Moustache took shotgun, and you sat in the back with My Linh. She looked like she was going to church, with a caramel wool dress that reached over her knees and a thin leather handbag meant for nothing but a diamond rosary. You wore a long-sleeved shirt to cover up the swelling on your arm from the botched tattoo removal.

You drove through the security gate, past rolling hills and stout trees that spat apples at the slightest breeze, parked in the circular drive, then walked on paving stones to the farmhouse. My Linh led the way and Sang hovered around her like a dragonfly, while you pulled the rear behind the Moustache, sidestepping free-range chickens pecking at the apples. There were three elders sitting on wooden chairs on the porch. You assumed one of them was Brother Number 1. My Linh dropped away from Sang and walked next to you, matching your pace in the rear, matching your slouch and, for all you knew, your rising heartbeat.

Brother Number 1 was dressed like a professor in chinos and a cardigan, but he had a boxer's face—pug-nosed, craggy, and pounded down to its ruby essence. He told the Moustache that he needed to eat more and Sang to eat less. He said it in English, maybe just for your benefit. Then he cut you with a smile. It was a slant carved into granite—deliberate and with permanent intent. He gave My Linh only a passing glance, told her to get the tea.

She got the steaming pot and cups from inside and served her father and the elders first, but then served you next. You felt everyone's eyes on you when she poured the cup in your hand, and then you felt the steam on your face like a wet kiss.

You spoke only when spoken to, though you were ready for all the questions — on why you wanted in on the core competencies, on how you were made to mission in grow-rips, on why you wanted to be a baller. But Brother Number 1 wasn't interested in talking about the business.

Instead, he told you about the harvest. About the different types of apples that they grew, about the different breeds of chicken that he had ordered from a catalogue — the Cornishes, the local Red Shavers, and even a Ga Noi special from Vietnam, looking like a hairless, itchy little buzzard. Then he showed you the grounds, walking you and the homies to the fenced-in garden with cabbages and carrots ready to be dug up. He showed you his new piglets, how'd they be gaining two pounds a day — almost as much as Sang, he said. He took a stick and poked around nooks of hay where the ducks had hidden their eggs.

Your homies disappeared around a turn, leaving you to follow Brother Number 1 with My Linh by your side, her face all demure and tilted down whenever her father spoke. He showed you the field for grazing cows and beside that the obstacle course that he lined with old tires. Then he showed you the engineered tree house among the giant maples that he had built for My Linh, that he had always promised her. He pointed up at the struts and bracings and said that back in Vietnam he had been a civil engineer. When he had finally finished the tree house, My Linh was too old for it, and now he knew it was for his grandchildren. He smiled at her when he said "grandchildren," and My Linh touched your shoulder and smiled at him, and it was like the two of them were talking to each other but using you as a prop.

Then they talked in Vietnamese like they were arguing, and then he gave you a two-fingered salute and left you two alone. My Linh took you to the greenhouse, her favourite spot on the farm. She liked the gush of pungent air that hit her face when she opened the double glass doors. Inside, you could smell a dozen tropical blooms—a small tamarind tree, dwarf bananas, a baby mangosteen tree, a lychee tree. Her father's treasures, she said, were the herbs, like the perilla with the leaves a rich purple on the underside, and a sharp and spicy taste of the kind you couldn't find at the T&T market.

Then she plucked a bunch of lychees. You followed her back to the farmhouse, through the back door, and up to a room with a bed covered with fluffy pink pillows and a couple of teddy bears lying on a puff pastry blanket. The room was mostly bare—no posters on the walls, no purple nighties oozing from the dresser drawers or tubes of lipstick in front of a glamour-bulb dressing mirror. Along the far wall there were beach balls lined row after row like headstones.

"My father decorated this place, not me," said My Linh. "When I was small and it was just us two at the refugee camp, I must have told him I wanted a beach ball, and he said he'd get me as many as I wanted. He didn't get around to it until he bought this farm, but by then I was, like, almost driving. I never sleep here."

My Linh told you to chill next to her on the puffy bed, since there was nowhere else to sit. You wondered how you and she could be alone with no one messing you up, what with her father sharking downstairs along with the homies with their brass and chains. She put a napkin between you and her, then the bunch of lychees on top. They were ripe, each the colour of a fading bruise, the flesh inside pressing against skin that looked tough and leathery but which she peeled off like new money.

"Just a snack before dinner," she said. She licked the juice from her fingers, then reached underneath her bed and pulled up a red Samsonite. She opened it and showed you fat stacks of scarlet-and-purple bills printed with tigers and sampans and temples.

South Vietnamese dong, she told you. They were her grandfather's life savings, a final bequest to her and only her that was now just Monopoly money. He died in a Communist re-education camp. This suitcase was her favourite thing in the world.

You felt the bed tilt towards her from the weight of the suitcase, and you puckered your lips and made your move. My Linh swerved her neck and your tongue ended up slick against her cheek. She clawed the back of your hand with her nails, making it look like you got a fresh five-dot tattoo.

"Straight-up, don't lose your focus," she said, then got up. She wanted to know what was up with dinner.

You followed her downstairs. Brother Number 1 was with the elders, along with Sang and the Moustache slouched in wooden chairs and cleaning out their teeth with toothpicks. Brother Number 1 said in English that there were leftovers for you two in the kitchen. My Linh planted her fists on her hips, said, "What gives? Why didn't you call us down?"

Her pops snorted, said, "You and your boy seemed busy," and then the two of them had it out in Vietnamese, her face turning as red as her father's. The Moustache lit a cigarette and Sang smiled at you like you were his next meal.

You excused yourself to take a piss and when you came back, Sang and the Moustache were gone.

"Come on," said My Linh, "I'll drive you home." She had the keys to a Porsche 911 parked next to the barn.

"That's you?" you said.

"Yeah, that's me," she said.

You had no idea she drove, never mind how she could handle the wet curves of Southeast Marine Drive in a 911 at night. You wanted to ask her what it was between her and her pops, and who dissed who by not sitting down together for dinner, but instead you said, "Sweet ride."

"I earned it," she said. Then she said, "Never mind the haters."

"I'm not a hater," you said.

"No," she said. "I'm telling you. To pay them no mind."

"Who are the haters?"

"The ones with small lives, of course. The ones with zero imaginations, who want your life because they can't think of how to live their own."

She pulled up to your grandfather's house and you felt like you were eleven again. You asked her if she wanted to hang out some more, but she said it was late, she needed to get home.

"To the farm?" you said.

"Shit no," she said. "My condo." You watched the back lights of her car from behind the blinds of the house.

That night you sweated your sheets wondering if you had somehow mortally offended Brother Number 1, but the next day you got the call to your first grow-rip. This was no mom-and-pop heist in the middle of the day. You hit these grows at night, in houses where no one slept.

During the rip you had crack ninjas who watched your behind, not a geezer like the Moustache or a poseur like Sang. These homies taught you how to use a silencer and night-vision goggles. Though you wondered if you needed any of that high-tech. The rival grows that you hit were ghetto affairs, wired like amateurs and less secure than a baby's bare ass. Coyote traps in plain view, doors with hook-and-eye locks that could be easily kicked in, droopy-eyed guard dogs, alarm systems that were easily suppressed. The plants themselves were subpar, and you believed that your mission was to rid humanity of this dank product.

That and the fat stacks, which you were soon rolling in after hitting a bunch of these rips. Enough so that you could no longer keep them in tins under your bed. Enough so that your mom and her boss looked at you cross-eyed with your shiny new threads and designer kicks. Enough so that you could tell your pops to screw off with trying to keep you in line. And before too long, enough to buy your own matte-painted Maserati.

When you got the call from My Linh to meet her for dinner, you put on your new Jordache jeans from the Bay and the collared shirt from Eaton's gentlemen's club section. It was early spring and the plum blossoms were out. You met My Linh at this Vietnamese noodle shop on Victoria Drive as the sun was nodding off. You sat across from her at a little table in the centre of the restaurant, which had mirrored walls like in a *Penthouse* spread. She wore a sleeveless blouse with these yellow print flowers, ironed crisp like a power suit. The other customers weren't the usual hyenas, but huddled quietly around their steaming bowls like a campfire in the rain. It was like they knew her, like they knew you.

The waitress gave you a once-over and asked My Linh for both your orders, like you were in My Linh's custody. "He can tell you what he wants," said My Linh.

You ordered the spicy Hue noodles. My Linh said,

"Back home in Vietnam, people ate noodles only at breakfast." Then she smiled and said, "That's why I like you. Outside you make me invisible and in here you make them come to me. With you I can be a chameleon or a peacock."

You asked her if that was why she brought you here.

"You've got game and you're my find," she said. When you didn't say anything, she told you about the filthy, noisy refugee camp in Hong Kong. She was eight, and it was just her and Brother Number 1 among hundreds in a warehouse. My Linh slept on top of her father in a table space like the one you were now sitting at. Her father cut a screen out of a cardboard box for a little privacy. Then he told her stories, and for the little while that he yarned, they were the only two in the world.

While My Linh talked, the other customers began emptying the restaurant. It was closing time. A young waitress slipped a bill on your table, and you reached for it. "I'm rolling now," you said.

My Linh took your hand off the bill, held it for a moment in her own. "I know," she said. "I'm the one cutting your stacks."

She left the bill on the table, told the girl to get more tea, got a dank potion in a smudged glass that she sipped like Cristal. The two of you sat until there was a tap on the front glass, and the girl went to the door to say that the shop was closed. "Keep your hands off the chain-lock," said My Linh. "They're with me."

In came your homies—the grow-rip ninjas. They slid past your table, lifted their hoods out of respect to My Linh but ignored your face, then settled in tables by the mirror walls. They weren't given menus. Instead, the girl's ma came out and started vacuuming around your feet. You lifted a leg to let the vacuum snout go under.

More of your homies came in, those you had known since you were a shorty under the school awning, all of them eyeballing you but giving nothing up, taking seats on the edges. The Moustache came in with Sang, who was the only one who gave you eyes.

Then someone turned off all the lights, except for a halogen tube right above your head. It felt like you were under a grow lamp.

Then the ma came to your table, told My Linh that the shop was closed. The ma was in tears, with her glitter-glam mascara all smudged.

"We're still hungry," said My Linh.

"No more food," said the ma.

"Then how about some tea at least," said My Linh.

The shop was now bumping with your homies, and with the girl and her ma busting their asses to get tea glasses for them all. All the homies drained their tea at the same time, and then they started banging their glasses on the tables with the same bongo drum rhythm. You felt like your head was about to shatter.

Then a man your pop's age came out from the kitchen with a fistful of cash that he laid out in front of My Linh. "There, you can go home now," he said, then crawled back to his corner with his sniffling wife and daughter.

My Linh counted the money, peeling each bill like it was lychee skin. "It's for his own good," she told you. "He pays us and we protect his shop."

"From what?" you said.

She smiled at you. "Trouble," she said.

"You're trouble," you said.

My Linh took a deep breath, then told you her favour-ite story from her father in the refugee camp: the Mayfly and the Glow-worm. "Once upon a time," she said, "the Mayfly asked the Glow-worm why the Glow-worm had a dim fire in its belly. When the Glow-worm told the Mayfly that it was the light that he lived by after the sun sets, the Mayfly looked pissed and confused, just like you right now. 'What do you mean?' said the Mayfly. 'The sun never sets. I've lived half my life and the sun is straight above our heads!' The Mayfly turned around, still pissed, and fluttered away from the Glow-worm. The Glow-worm didn't have the heart to tell the Mayfly about sunsets.

"I used to always cry when I heard that story," said My Linh.

You said you didn't get it.

"Mayflies only live for a day," she said, but you still didn't get it. Then you asked My Linh straight-up, what had she brought you here for?

"You want to be a Face, don't you?" she said.

You said you didn't get it, and anyway that was for Brother Number 1 to decide.

She looked like you had just thrown water in her face. "You're wrong," she said. "You're my inheritance. All of you are."

You got up.

"You leave when I say so," said My Linh.

Sang made a kissing sound behind you as you busted out the front door. With no ride, you took the bus home.

A few nights later, the Moustache and Sang knocked on the window outside your bedroom, woke you up, and pulled you out for a grow-rip. "Just like old times," said the Moustache. You said that they weren't qualified to be ripping grows. "Then show us the way," said the Moustache. It was straight-up an order from HQ.

They still rolled in a beat-up old car. During the day you wouldn't have noticed the wheezing muffler, but now at night the car made a mess of a noise. Still, the giddy flash of their yellow teeth in the shadows was contagious, and being with them took you back to old times — to the candy store beside your old school, to the cracked asphalt courts.

Your destination was a crack shack on East 22nd with a pit bull sign and no lights. Your homies didn't have any tech with them, no night-vision goggles, no gun and silencer, just a crowbar to scratch open the back door. With a single twist from Sang the door yielded like butter. "We have already cased this joint out," said the Moustache.

Inside there were no traps or alarms that tripped off. Just darkness, and then Sang's flashlight beam on pot after pot of second-rate bud. "Too easy," said Sang, as he cut the stalks with a machete and stuffed them in a canvas bag.

The Moustache tossed you a canvas bag and told you that the next door had more plants. Too easy was your thought too. You went into the room by yourself and the homies closed the door behind you. You flicked a switch and there were the shivering tendrils of weed begging for you to take them. It looked like a little boy's bedroom, with silverfish scurrying on the floor over a balsa wood airplane and a bunch of deflated balls. You forgot about the plants when you saw the posters on the wall. The greatest ballers of the day were staring right at you: Michael Jordan, Isaiah Thomas, Dominique Wilkins.

And that's when you heard the popping of the Moustache's muffler in the distance, and then a fainter but rising bark of a dog. You tried to open the bedroom door, but it was locked from the other side. You kicked the door but it would not yield. You turned off the lights and saw the glimmer of bodies out in the yard, throwing up shadows through the shut blinds. All you could think of was the lavender smell of your mother's bookmarks and the clean smell of static whenever your father was close. Now you heard the shuffling of steel-toed boots in the next room, the bark of the dog. How could they abandon you? You weren't just a baller, you were the MVP. You despaired that in the faces of the strangers who were coming for you, that you would not see your homies in them, but rather something more like your own.

The Abalone Diver

Winter is the best time to harvest mandarin oranges on Jeju Island, and Thuy cannot escape the smell of them. She works alongside her husband, plucks the small fruit with her bare hands, brushing off snow, the oranges half-buried in white. It is so cold that the green leaves tremble. She stubbornly refuses to wear gloves despite Jun's suggestions. Her hands turn a red so deep that when, working in haste, her palm gets pricked by the shears, the blood is just a darker shade of her skin. Drops of it speckle the snow. The whole collage — all the colours obscenely vivid in their contrast — reminds her of the red, white, green, and orange ice desserts she had in Vietnam, although then it was the orange of mango.

The skies are a whitish blue, cloudless, but the air is so cold that the sun seems unreal, merely a painting over the horizon line of the East China Sea. By day's end there are still so many oranges left on the trees that they multiply the sunset through the leaves. They are working too slowly, and will need more pickers than the two farmhands they have now. When it is dark, husband and wife retreat inside their home, heat rising from the floorboards as if from the centre of the earth. She washes the crusted blood off her hands so as to tend to dinner. Jun must be tired — he does not help her as he usually insists on doing. She steams his favourite type of rice, a rustic purple as if bruises have been mixed in. Dried fish, kimchi, and seaweed on the side. When dinner is over, Jun settles into the couch with the television on, but not her favourite soap opera, the one that she sometimes holds responsible for taking her to this country. So she puts on her winter jacket and a broad-rimmed hat, slips out the back door for a walk. She never wore clothes so heavy back in Vietnam. Jun does not say a thing when she leaves. He is not that type of husband.

She walks down to the sea. The smell of oranges is still present, as if embedded inside her nostrils. The sea is never very far away no matter where she is on this island. She heads to the cove that belongs to the *haenyeo*, the old mermaids. She steps off a path worn down by tourists and clambers down jagged rock beaten over by the waves. It is a volcanic rock that glints more brightly with reflected moonlight than during the day, when its blackness sucks up all the sun.

Right now there is not another soul in the cove. The air is heavy with a salt that stabs Thuy's lungs, and then the sound of pounding waves wipes away all other sensation. She comes down to a flat landing by a small pool of standing water, protected on the far side by a sheer slab of rock that takes the brunt of the waves. It is here where she takes off her winter jacket, her hat and shoes, and strips down to her underwear. Her bare skin feels electrified. When Thuy was a child in Vietnam, she swam in the brown streams of her village and in the sparkling South China Sea. She was older, in high school, when she entered an indoor pool for the first time, and the feeling of completely still water clothing her body was a revelation, like touching a sleeping beast in captivity. She became a competitive swimmer in high school, which was not so long ago.

She jumps in feet first, the sharp teeth of frigid water tearing into her skin. Somehow she manages this thought: the East and South China Sea, though separated by thousands of kilometres, are really one body and therefore this moment is tied to her childhood despite the gaping passage of time. As she is swallowed up by this acid chill, this is both a feat of the imagination, and the truth.

She is immersed in the sea for only a moment, but when she emerges, she feels whole and new. Only briefly, though, before the greater chill of damp air and dissipated adrenalin settles in. She has also brought a small towel, snuck inside her winter jacket. When she gets back home, her husband is reading a book. She does not read Korean and so has no idea what the book is about. She has the broad-rimmed hat on and Jun does not know of her damp hair beneath. She does not get close enough for him to smell the brine on her.

"Exploration?" he says, a coarse finger caressing the thin spine, a smile that is still bashful across his broad face though they have been married for almost a year. This is how they communicate mostly, in their mutually cumbersome English, one word at a time. Jun has recently taken to wearing a thin baby-blue scarf around his neck, his indoor scarf.

"Yes," she says. "Exploration."

...

In Vietnam, both Thuy and her mother loved watching Korean soap operas. Mostly from pirated DVDs that Thuy bought for a discount from the village market where both she and her mother worked, her mother in a dry goods kiosk and Thuy for whatever monger could fit her school and swimming schedule. Most Korean soaps were mega miniseries consisting of twenty hours of television or so, but Thuy's absolute favourite was *Moonlight Nocturne*, which went on for countless hours over several seasons. It featured a lead named Sung who was handsome and slender, with floppy hair that grew over his ears and touched his brows. He was a wealthy orphan who lived in a large mansion by the sea. Somehow, losing his parents at a young age and being left with nothing but his good looks and a vast sum of wealth did not make Sung callous and cold-hearted, but quite the opposite. He was unwittingly charming and funnelled the energy from his pangs of loss into good causes. He was also perhaps too open-hearted to his myriad lady friends, who drove the plot of each episode by conniving against each other for his attentions. He wore colourful scarves that made him seem even more sensitive. The quality of the pirated DVDs varied wildly—at least with regard to the reproduction and the dubbing—but never the quality of the storylines and acting.

Thuy and her mother would watch these DVDs in their hut just outside the village, beside rice paddies owned by one of her mother's uncles. They used to live in a larger house on their own farm until the Communist government seized the land for a multiplex development. When that happened, Thuy's father shot the local cadre member who was in charge of urban planning and then shot himself. Thuy's parents had always intended to spare their daughter from a life spent on haunches in the rice paddies, but the seizure almost ensured her a life of menial labour of one sort or another. During high school Thuy worked in the kiosks when she wasn't studying or swimming the butterfly in competitions. Often after school she would go help her mother close the dry goods kiosk for the evening, and both women would sneak glances at the little television set that was mounted high on a wooden shelf, watching one of the Korean DVDs.

...

It is a bright Sunday the next time Thuy comes down to the mermaids' cove. A day of church and rest from the harvest. On past Sundays, Jun has taken Thuy hiking up

Mount Halla, or to visit the ancient lava rock huts held together by a clay and barley stalk mortar, or to the pine and rose mazes—the places where honeymooners from all over South Korea go. Now she heads down to the cove by herself. She sees some of the mermaids returning with their catch for the day, letting out sharp whistles as they break the surface of the water. They emerge in smooth black wetsuits that give ageless form to their bodies, some thin, some portly, but all with strong thighs and robust biceps. They take to the small beach like calm seals, with their nets, their bowl-shaped floats and weeding hoes. The youngest of them is in her sixties.

Instead of clambering down the cliffside rocks, Thuy takes the wooden steps that the tourists use. During the summertime the cove is infested with visitors, but in the winter the mermaids are left unbothered. Thuy walks past rows of plastic red buckets filled with sea cucumbers, the water trembling at the lips of the buckets. The cucumbers within seem like squirming red caterpillars, water-swollen and huge. Winter is their season.

On this day the waves are not as violent as they were the last night she was here, though the water is almost as dark as the volcanic rock. Thuy skips over a few sharp rocks to the same flat landing by the same calm pool. She takes off her clothes. She is wearing her bathing suit beneath, the shimmering aqua-blue Spandex. Some of the mermaids look up from whatever it is they are doing—removing flippers, untangling nets. Some of them cluck their tongue against the roof of their mouth in disapproval. The tide is lower this time, and when Thuy jumps in feet first, the water reaches only halfway up her thigh, just above her knees. She has to bend her limbs low to get shoulder deep. Before her chin breaks the surface of the water, one of the mermaids pulls her up by the shoulders from behind, as if to save her from drowning. Thuy shakes her head at first, but in the end lets the old woman pull her back onto the flat rock. The mermaid still has her diving mask on, the tempered glass surrounding the woman's oval face, the rubber hood thick over her ears so that Thuy is not sure if the woman can hear her. She wouldn't understand the Vietnamese that Thuy is speaking anyway, which is the only true way that Thuy knows how to ask this: to be allowed in the water, to be a mermaid too.

...

Thuy met her husband through a matchmaker. Not the traditional kind, those old ladies who dotted the villages and who knew all the local gossip and who the dependable astrologers were. Instead, Thuy and Jun were matched by VietSeoul. The company was based in Seoul, according to its bilingual Korean-Vietnamese website, and was affiliated with a finishing school in Ho Chi Minh City that taught Vietnamese girls how to be good Korean wives. Make sure that the rice is on the left side and the soup on the right side when setting up the table. That sort of thing.

It was Thuy's mother who forwarded the VietSeoul link. Now that Thuy was done with high school but could not afford to leave home for university, what was she going to do?

"You can work with me in the market for the rest of your life," said her mother. "Or you can find your own Sung."

Thuy received the VietSeoul e-newsletter that included testimonials of happy couples and passwords for the next matchmaking sessions in Ho Chi Minh City. When she signed up for one of the sessions, she was emailed the photos and bios of the Korean men who would be attending. Jun's short bio simply gave his name, listed Jeju Island as his home, Christianity as his religion, and "land development" as his profession. His photo was in colour but was grainy due to a poor scanning job. It was of a man in his early to mid-twenties in naval dress uniform, a stiff white-gloved hand in salute, not quite touching the black brim of his white hat. She showed her mother the photos of Jun and two other bachelors.

"Handsome," her mother said, without specifying which one. Thuy thought Jun was handsome enough from his photo, with a square jaw and a soft curl of the lips belying an otherwise severe military expression, although she wanted to see him without his hat to make sure.

Her mother went with Thuy on the two-hour bus ride to Ho Chi Minh City. The matchmaking session wasn't until the evening, but her mother insisted on leaving in the morning. She wanted time to buy Thuy a proper evening dress and to visit a hair salon, so that Thuy would have the same highlights in her hair that the soap stars had.

How uncomfortable Thuy felt in Ho Chi Minh City. And it wasn't just a matter of being a peasant dodging the choking rivers of motorbikes. The metropolis rang false to her. It seemed that new skyscrapers were sprouting up every day in order to cast the old colonial villas in their shadows, or at least the villas that were not already torn down. And all this progress was made in order to ape other places where bigger lives played out. As with the gaudy glass buildings, it was the same with the imitation pop music and soap operas that they made there. Ho Chi Minh City could kill off old Saigon, but it would never be Seoul.

In District 7 they bought a cicada-green dress at the Lotte Mart, the Korean shopping chain. Thuy walked out of the mall wearing it while her mother carried her old clothes in a plastic bag. "Overpriced, but maybe you'll earn it," said her mother, smiling.

In the evening, they went together to the nightclub where the meeting would take place. The highball glasses, the strobe lights, the bar stools—television had made such an establishment familiar. On the wall were glowing murals of cats with whiskers made out of some luminous plastic material, thin strands of light protruding out of flat surfaces.

One of the marriage brokers was standing outside the door to a private room. He was a short, brusque man who wore a name tag with a Vietnamese name but who spoke the language with a broken Korean accent. He gave Thuy her name tag and motioned her mother to wait at the bar.

"Take as much time as you need," said Thuy's mother. "Don't worry about me."

Inside the private room, three bachelors were hunched together on a lounge sofa on one side of a long table, while a dozen women sat pressed against each other on the other side. On the table were plastic bottles of water. Thuy took a quick glance at the women—girls really, around her age, all villagers. Thuy shouldn't have been surprised; was she expecting big-city girls with university degrees?

When she saw Jun in profile, she thought it was his father. The salt in his hair glittered in the track lighting and deep grooves were worn into the laugh lines of his face. He wore a black blazer over a black turtleneck, which made him look even older. All the Korean men would have been her father's age, if he had still been alive.

The broker clapped his hands together to get everyone's attention. "Mingle, please," he said in Vietnamese, and then spoke for an extended period in Korean to the men. Jun turned to Thuy and presented her with a full smile, all lips, the smile that his military photo only hinted at. Thuy ran out the door.

Her mother was at the bar nursing a small cup of tea.

"Were they being mean to you so soon?" she said. When Thuy explained to her what she had seen, her mother dabbed her daughter's tears with a napkin. "Don't act so surprised. A mature man is for the best. Now, stop ruining your mascara."

Thuy returned to the private room. The other girls were frozen in place on the couches until one of the men sidled over to talk to them, at which point the girl would come alive, tilt her ear towards the man like a plant to the sun. The men took turns speaking to the girls according to ground rules that weren't shared with the Vietnamese, hopping from seat to seat like frogs on lily pads. There were only two translators, who buzzed above the couches to where they were needed most.

Jun took his time talking to one girl then another while Thuy sat silently. Beneath all her feelings—of fear, excitement, disappointment, and pity—was a keening hunger. Thuy had eaten only a couple of small, sticky rice cakes during the bus ride. Finally a waiter brought in some appetizers, small plates of tiny salted shrimp strategically spread across the table. Thuy picked up as many shrimp as she could with three fingers and tossed them into her mouth, the shrimp spreading across the surface of her tongue along with the melting salt. The pleasure of the salt and protein did not dim her pain, nor did the pain detract from the pleasure of the shrimp. These feelings simply coexisted, distinct and intense at the same moment, with the integrity of their forms intact. Another man sat next to her and smiled, spreading a Korean-Vietnamese dictionary flat on the table like a road map.

Jun and Thuy did not speak to each other until near the end of the night. By then things had loosened up and alcohol was brought to the table to fan the volume in the room like a flame. Jun stood out from the other two men with their starched white shirts and silk ties, who clearly enjoyed being fawned over by a dozen women. She liked that Jun looked bored. A couple of the girls next to her were asking a broker how long the men were staying in the city. The broker said not long, they were heading to Hue the next morning to interview more women before making a decision. Thuy could hear the gasps from the girls. Women from Hue were famously beautiful. The broker checked his notes and corrected himself. Hanoi, not Hue. "Hanoi girls have buckteeth and horse faces," one of the girls assured the others. "They stew cats." Again a gasp, but this time it seemed more from relief. The girls begged the broker not to speak a word to the Korean men about Hue.

A cocktail glass shattered on the floor and all the voices jelled into a single laugh before breaking up again. In all of this Jun and Thuy found a bubble of silence to hide in until one of the brokers came. The broker made no effort to mitigate the awkwardness, taking his time to chew on Jun's words before passing them on to Thuy in processed Vietnamese.

"What did he say?" said Thuy to the broker. "Why is he smiling?"

"He says you must be very hungry, you are the only girl eating the food," said the broker. "He says he will order you anything you want."

"More shrimp," said Thuy.

In the end it took a sophomoric question from Jun, "What books have you read recently?"—something likely straight out of the instruction manual for potential Korean grooms—to provoke a sneer from Thuy when she answered, "*War and Peace.*"

"You speak English?" said Jun. He was speaking directly to her now.

Thuy nodded.

"I do not believe you."

"I am speaking English now."

"No, the *War and Peace.* Your English cannot be that good."

"Okay, then," said Thuy. "How about *Anne of Green Gables*?"

"I can believe that," said Jun. "*Anne of Green Gables* is for every high school girl."

Thuy lowered her head at that reminder of their respective ages, and she gave him credit for sensing his indiscretion.

"I have read it too," he said. "Not too long ago."

"There is only the English version here in Vietnam," she said.

"Do you know what the 'kindred spirit' means? It is mentioned often in the story."

"Strange term! It means best friends, no?"

"In Korean version it means friendly ghost."

"That must be incorrect."

"Incorrect," repeated Jun. "I mean that I agree."

She let out a small giggle. It felt like a subversive thing they were doing, speaking directly to each other. The broker left the two of them alone. Thuy's broken English was better than Jun's, and he often hesitated at the edge of a thought, grasping for the right word—his uncertainty bridging their age gap. He was more quiet than the other men and preferred not to talk about himself. Thuy credited him with humility. Only when he spoke of Jeju Island did he become excited. When there was a term that was missing from his vocabulary (*octopus*, say, or *subterranean lava*), he reached into his blazer pocket for his Samsung phone. He had installed a translation app.

He preferred listening to Thuy rather than talking about himself, tensing his jaw in empathy at appropriate moments. Thuy had thought she was more of a listener herself, but now she enjoyed unspooling her broken English without thought to how she sounded. She had never had such an audience with an older man. She felt reckless with her stream-of-consciousness meanderings, about the omnipresence of coconuts in her village and working in the market, about her mother, though she never mentioned her father and Jun did not ask. She felt like a child again, swimming in any direction in the ocean instead of being tied to the straight lines of the competitive pool. She noticed that Jun was missing a side molar, but she didn't mind.

She thought she had gone too far when she mentioned her favourite television show. She was so relieved when Jun said that he watched *Moonlight Nocturne* as well, and then gobsmacked when Jun told her that in fact it was filmed on Jeju Island. Then she confessed her infatuation with Sung. Jun began to say something in English but once again couldn't find the words. He pulled out his app and typed something, then handed her the phone.

The screen read: "You are in love with this character, but he is not real."

"I know that, that is okay," she said, looking Jun in the eyes.

The next morning, when Thuy woke up on her old mat in her old hut, on her floor of pounded dirt, Jun's spirit was a faint mist that disappeared in the light. All Thuy could remember was his missing molar and the lines on his face when he smiled. When she confided in her mother that she did not think she could go through with this, her mother told her not to be a coward.

...

They had two weddings, one in her village and one on Jeju Island. The wedding in Vietnam was in December and was sparsely attended. Her mother was there, along with her mother's uncle, a couple of distant cousins, a few friends from high school. Thuy suspected that most of the villagers were scared off by anything even distantly connected with her late father, fearing that the authorities would be aroused, though the Catholic priest who officiated let them use the village church for free. The priest was used to butting heads with the cadres and regarded the wedding as an act of subversion, however small.

The small procession made the inside of the church feel enormous. Jun wore a dove-grey suit with polished black shoes. Thuy wore a simple wedding dress that her mother had bought from the village market, its most extravagant feature a pair of lace gloves with little white bows fastened at the wrists. Everyone else wore knitted sweaters or nylon jackets against an unusual chill. The inside of the church was drafty, its upkeep neglected when the Communists choked off funding to the parish. Monkeys bounded outside, casting shadows resembling arched-back cats through the stained-glass windows. Then they started infiltrating the inside of the walls in search of warmth. Thuy couldn't see the monkeys, but she could hear their laughter, making the timber walls vibrate as she and Jun exchanged vows. When she swam in the rivers as a child, she would hear the monkeys cheer her on, see them above in the boughs of the jackfruit trees while she did the backstroke. Now their cackling cheered her again, made her family seem larger.

After they exchanged vows, Jun faced Thuy's mother, got on his knees, and bowed so low that his forehead touched the ground. His pant leg cuffs pulled up and Thuy could see his socks. There was a wedding cake and a bottle of red wine, though not enough glasses and so the guests shared.

Jun left first for Korea to prepare for the second wedding, and later that spring Thuy flew for the first time. Everyone at the airport on Jeju Island seemed to be either middle-aged men with golf clubs or young couples with matching sweaters and neon-bright sneakers. Honeymooners, Jun would later tell her.

Thuy wore the same dress for her Korean wedding. Instead of a church, this wedding took place in a glass high-rise. Another bride was exiting the same revolving door that Thuy entered. In the lobby she found the posters of the couples getting married that day, and the one of her and Jun was framed by a heart with a time and room number stamped on the top corner.

She proceeded alone down an aisle that was more like a catwalk, with strobe lights and dry ice smoking up the runway and the heads of diners beneath the haze. There were flashing bulbs, massive television screens on every wall. Jun waited for her at the end of the aisle with his wide smile, never showing his teeth, wearing a pair of bright white gloves like a valet. Diners looked up from their steaming plates at the monitors so that they didn't have to turn their heads to the altar.

Afterwards, she cut the cake with a long knife, more like a sword, never getting to taste it before being hustled by the woman with a headset from table to table, where Thuy was embraced by complete strangers. It took only thirty minutes in total before she was returned to the lobby with her new husband. They stood at a table with a small gathering of their gift envelopes, each with money inside. Jun wore a stalwart expression while he fingered the cards and glanced at the other tables, where people were collecting much larger piles of envelopes. Thuy daydreamed about the taste of wedding cake.

...

Thuy waits until after the orange harvest is over, when she can claim a morning for herself, before she tries to make it down to the cove again. A warm spring morning, when the rocks take on a gentler, silver cast. When she gets to the bottom of the stairs, tourists are standing along the shore taking photographs. The mermaids are already beneath the sea — all except for one, a skinny old woman with her wetsuit on but without the cowl. The tourists take pictures of this *haenyeo* while she stands among them, a head shorter.

When the old *haenyeo* catches Thuy's eyes, she smiles. Her face is a set of craggy vertical lines and appears to be made of the same stuff as this island. Thuy had come bearing a request in Korean, but in her nervousness she cannot form the words. Instead she says,

"Annyeonghaseyo," the standard greeting, the only Korean she can conjure at the moment despite being enrolled in a language class for months now.

The *haenyeo* pricks her ears up at the slant in Thuy's accent. "Ni hao ma!" she says.

Thuy shakes her head. She is not Mandarin. "Beteunam-ui," Thuy says, pointing to herself. Vietnamese.

The mermaid shakes her head as well. "Beteunam-ui, non," she says. "Zhunguo. Nihon-go. Deutsch, Francais, oui."

The tourists say something in German to the *haenyeo*, hard consonants falling from the fair sky, and she answers back in German, clapping her cotton-gloved hands. They laugh at what must be a joke.

"How about English?" says Thuy.

At this the *haenyeo* smiles. "Of course, English."

By now some of the other mermaids have raised their heads out of the water. They recognize Thuy and start saying something that Thuy does not understand.

"Oh, you are the one who wants to dive with us," says the *haenyeo*, her eyes disappearing into the lines of her smile.

Thuy nods. The old woman has taken the one wish Thuy had come bearing, somehow has returned it to her stronger, more real. "Yes, I do," says Thuy.

"Cha, don't you care about your life?"

...

During her first year on Jeju Island, she saw ponies. Silver-maned and small enough to ride under low-hanging fruit trees. As ubiquitous as the plodding water buffaloes back home, but dreamier, like moonlight. They could be seen grazing on both sides of the road, at the end of every curve.

During her first year she saw honeymooners all over the island, with matching T-shirts, standing under waterfalls. Thuy hated to be one of them at first, but Jun wanted his neighbours to see them like this. They took long hikes up Mount Halla, where they would pass hale elders using ski poles on the wooden steps. They had sunset picnics on the ancient fortress wall, which had once protected the island against the invading Mongolians. They visited the volcanic stone *dol hareubang* statues with phallic noses and vaginal lips.

Jun had lived alone just before she moved here, although he had been with his mother until she had died a year earlier, had been his mother's boy for almost all his life. During Thuy's first year in his home they mostly had sex, cooked, and worked on the orange farm. Of these things, it was the cooking that most surprised her. The kitchen was the one place where she had expected to be left alone. When Jun was there, it was at first to teach her how to prepare raw fish or to make kimchi, and she thought that after she learned these things she would be left to her own devices. But he insisted on being in the kitchen even when she had obtained this competence, just as he was always by her side in the market and in the orange fields. Even when she made him Vietnamese dishes, he insisted on helping her or just standing over her while she chopped. He always helped her clear the table before they retired to the living room to watch TV. He told her he was not that kind of husband, though he didn't explain what other kinds there were. Every month he mailed a letter to Thuy's mother, a small red envelope inside the larger envelope.

During the first year he showed her the *jokbo*, the lineage books of his family. The books lined two shelves at the bottom of his bookcase. He pulled out a volume in the middle of the shelf where he had the thin pages earmarked. Here was a *yangban*, a mandarin, here was a naval officer. He moved his fingers down the centuries. Here was a doctor, here was a shipbuilder. Then, cracking one of the newer spines, he showed her the name of the first mandarin orange farmer in the family. He picked up the final volume and turned to the last page, which had Chinese characters, pointed to the blank space where their son's name would go. He had a thought that he couldn't speak in English, so he reached for his phone. "Our family started with our heads in the clouds, then moved down to the sea, and now here we are close to the earth," said the screen.

"Your head is still in the clouds," said Thuy.

During the first year she was mistaken for a prostitute twice while walking with Jun in the evening on the boardwalk, and Jun got into one fist fight defending her honour.

During the first year she met his friends, farmers his age or even older with yellowed teeth who spoke not a word of English. They would come to play a card game that Jun called Go-Stop. It seemed like such a dainty game for men, with little red cards that were just larger than a thumbprint depicting cranes, chrysanthemums, and other animals and flowers on one side. When these men came over, she was finally left alone in the kitchen, coming out only to bring them snacks made out of cracked wheat and dry seaweed, or to serve bottomless amounts of *soju* that Jun had chilled in the freezer. Once she had made a crack about these men needing to drink so much to play a little girl's game, lining these little cards side by side. It was the first time that Jun had ever told her to shut up, then drew in his breath and explained to her that it was gambling, and therefore as manly as smoking or drinking *soju*. After a certain hour in the night his friends openly leered at her with the tips of their tongues jutting through the gaps in their teeth, and sometimes slapped her ass as she served them snacks. Jun would snort alcohol out through his nose at the sight.

In that first year she met Jun's aunt who lived on a neighbouring farm. The aunt wore a purple shawl and nodded silently when Thuy was in the same room, but never spoke directly to her. Thuy thought the aunt spent most of her time complaining about her, though Jun would never really explain what his aunt had said. The aunt sometimes brought over some old local wench or another to talk to Jun.

"Why is she still trying to introduce you?" asked Thuy.

"Her bad habit," Jun explained to Thuy with his smile.

After the first year she took birth control, keeping the dial of little pills hidden deep within her cluttered purse. And after that year there were no more ponies. Horses were still everywhere on the island, but Thuy no longer noticed them.

...

This time the skinny old *haenyeo*—her name is Yuri—is expecting her. The other mermaids started their dives at around nine in the morning, so Yuri told Thuy to come out a little later, when the others would be busy in the sea. At the top of the cliff is a ramshackle change room where Yuri has set aside a black wetsuit. The suit is a little short, and Thuy has to stretch the rubber against her spine as she pulls the sleeves over her shoulders. She walks stiffly at first, but the rubber is worn and soon yields to her form. "Is it one of yours?" Thuy asks. Yuri is much shorter, with bones as thin as a bird's. Thuy could never fit into something of Yuri's.

"My older sister's," says Yuri. "But don't worry, she won't be asking for it. She drowned a few years ago in that same suit."

Yuri buckles a set of square metal weights around her own waist. Then she reaches for Thuy's arm. "Help me down the steps, will you? These weights are going to crush my knees."

"Where are mine?"

"You don't need them. Not yet. You stay in the shallow water."

When they reach the bottom of the cove, the other mermaids are all underwater. Thuy can only see their floating orange baskets, the *taewak*. There are already tourists taking photographs. "You're late!" says one of the tourists to Yuri. "We thought you had drowned."

"Still alive!" says Yuri. She starts chatting with the group from South Africa. Yuri's walking is laboured, but when she is waving her arms she is a stationary sprite, petrified from the waist down. She points the tourists to another old lady on her haunches beside a series of red buckets, the day's early catch of periwinkles and abalone. "Good deal, good deal!" she says.

Thuy does not have the chance to set foot in the water by the time the other mermaids emerge at the shore, heralded by the slapping against rock of wet flippers. Their suits are bright orange at the torso, which makes Thuy think of an angry mob of mandarins. Yuri stands between them and Thuy. "Stay behind me," she says.

Yuri and the others are yelling at each other, their flying spittle mimicking the ocean spray. Although Thuy does not understand a word, the lines of argument are completely clear. The mermaids would have continued to yell at each other except that more tourists are gathering on the platform. With two claps Yuri breaks their collective fever. The mermaids need to gather in front of the tourists to chant their prayer before diving into the water again. The show must go on.

"You come back tomorrow," says Yuri to Thuy. "Those old women don't know this, but they need you." She explains that because the *haenyeo* are a dying breed, their daughters preferring not to continue the profession, they need young blood like Thuy. "Beggars can't be choosers," says Yuri. Thuy wonders if Yuri picked up that proverb from one of the tourists.

"Why are their wetsuits orange?" says Thuy.

"The government recently issued them," says Yuri. "They think it will be easier for the coast guard to find a drowned body. Smart, no?"

...

Thuy has met some of the other Vietnamese brides on this island. Once a month they gather in a café or during the summer for a picnic. They have a favourite spot on a hill overlooking one of the inactive volcanic calderas, now a verdant concave green. They are the group wearing sun hats and sweaters in the summer while everyone around them is in shorts. When the Vietnamese wives get together, they are boisterous in their merriment and their frustrations. It is a reminder of how quiet they have otherwise become in this new world. Over summer rolls stuffed with prawns they pass around tips on where the best rice paper is sold or how to cope with having no

Vietnamese fish sauce because only the darker, heavier Korean variety is available. What to do when you can't find fresh turmeric. Tips on the best health clinics—who the most sympathetic doctors and nurses are.

At these picnics the brides wring their hands over their decision to come to this island, or the decision that was made for them. They make the predictable complaints about how disappointed they are in their husbands, which broadens into observations about how strange the Koreans are—eating live octopus, the tentacles still squirming on their lips and between their teeth. The brides know a little about Jun, and some are jealous at what they perceive is his attentiveness and chivalry. They express this jealousy in different ways. Some focus on the failings of their own husbands, while some bend a wrist to show Thuy the jewellery that their husbands have bought for them.

They exchange macabre tales. There was something in the news not so long ago about a Vietnamese wife who was murdered by her husband, thrown over a twentieth-storey balcony. This followed a few months after a similar story. They comfort themselves with reports that those men suffered a mental disability of some sort. Those were not normal husbands.

Thuy sometimes thinks about how the earth yielded itself so much more easily back home, at least in some ways. She remembers spring mornings on the white beaches outside her village. Back home the old women didn't dive for shellfish. Instead, it seems, they just sat cross-legged on the beach during low tide, as if in meditation, the sand raked smooth by the last night's waves. Wearing silk trousers and conical hats to keep their faces in shade, they would simply flap their legs, beating gently on the sand with their knees. The clams would emerge by themselves from beneath the ground, awakened by the rhythm, their shells as white as the sand. There to be picked up with bare hands.

Thuy only half-listens to her new sisters. Usually she feels that she has nothing in common with these women other than a language and some other touchstones — books they've read or music they've listened to — memories of which, she fears, will all fade away. Sometimes, though, one of them will make a certain face or bend her fingers a certain way and Thuy will for a moment believe that she is among her old friends. There was one girl who reminded her a little bit of her friend Diep, another swimmer. This girl didn't have the mien of a swimmer, but there was something about her expression — that same modest frown in the face of victory.

This girl, whom Thuy called Little Diep, was a bit of a philosopher. She tried to sow the idea among the wives that they were like the Vietnamese expatriates of old — nationalists like Phan Boi Chau and Ho Chi Minh who rallied the Vietnamese against French colonialization from the outside. Phan Boi Chau left for Japan, from where in 1905 he published *History of the Loss of Vietnam*, in which his lament — that the greatest human suffering comes from the loss of one's country — was a clarion call for resistance. The book became a touchstone in Vietnam's wars for independence. Ho Chi Minh left Vietnam to study Marxism in Paris and Moscow before returning home to liberate the country. Little Diep said that they, the wives, were the heirs to this spirit of independence, patriotism, and cosmopolitanism.

The other women laughed and flicked lime juice on the girl's face to douse her reverie. "We are not here to save our country," they said, "only to make our Korean husbands happy and to send back money to our parents."

Little Diep only came to a few of their picnics and then disappeared. Thuy assumed the girl must have got pregnant. Until a Vietnamese bride got pregnant on Jeju, she lived a life of pure fantasy, and once she had a baby, her life here became real and she would disappear from the group. It was as if their group was a kind of purgatory until they passed on to the next world — to heaven or hell, Thuy wasn't sure. The mothers who disappeared were replaced by brides who had just arrived. It wouldn't be long before Thuy became one of the longest-serving veterans of these picnics.

Of course, there were snickers of satisfaction among the other wives when Little Diep disappeared. Her reveries comparing them to heroes of old were all talk, they said. Yet, since she left, someone else sometimes mentioned Ho Chi Minh and Phan Boi Chau, as if the conversation was never finished. "The difference between Ho Chi Minh and Phan Boi Chau and us is that those men eventually went back home," said one of the wives.

"We are here to stay, and if one of us runs home, it is because she has been defeated by Korea and takes nothing of benefit back with her."

...

Yuri refuses to allow Thuy to put on diving weights. Thuy is to keep her body parallel to the surface of the earth, and to stay in shallow water. The shallows are usually reserved for the eldest *haenyeo*, but Yuri assures them that Thuy is not after their catch. Instead of diving for octopus or abalone, Thuy is given shears to reap the seaweed that sways near the surface. She carries the bundled seaweed on her back, up glistening rocks to dry land. After a few weeks of this, she loses all patience. Yuri reluctantly hands her a belt.

That these old women think they are better swimmers incenses Thuy. She can easily outpace every single one of them to the horizon line. That is, until she loses her breath. Thuy has the muscles of a pony, but she does not have the lungs of a mermaid. The old *haenyeo* swim without oxygen tanks and must hold their breath underwater. As fast as Thuy is, the darting octopus will forever stay just beyond the reach of her spear because she does not have that one necessary tool: patience. And neither will the abalone at the bottom of the ocean yield to her. By the time these old women settle themselves thirty feet under the sea, upside down and mulling about from rock to rock as if they are in the aisles of a grocery store, Thuy

can take it no more and has to dart up for air. Yuri takes
back her belt.

...

Jun is not one to forbid her from doing anything. Instead,
he expresses his worries for her. "You're not safe with
them," he says.

"I have been swimming in the ocean all of my life."

"I don't mean the ocean." In a stammer he reaches for
his phone. "The old *haenyeo*, they are not like us. They
are set in their ways."

"How do you know?"

"I've known most of them since I was a boy. The world
keeps moving, and they are stubborn, to be left behind."

"I don't understand."

"They have a death wish."

"They do not."

He will not forbid her, but when fear does not work,
he will speak of his dreams. His dream, for instance, of
working side by side with her on the orange farm.

"I will still be here, especially for the harvest season,"
she says.

Jun tells her there is so much for them to do on the
orange farm all year round, even when it is not the harvest season. "Because you are gone every morning, I will
have to hire an extra hand," he says.

"I will make money as a diver. The *haenyeo* have put their
children through university with the money they make."

"How long will I have to wait?" says Jun, and Thuy no longer knows if Jun is talking about money.

During her first days on Jeju Island, Jun took her to the mansion where the character Sung lived in *Winter Nocturne*. It has been years since the last episode was filmed there, and the mansion has become a pilgrimage site, one of the few famous houses on the island that is not made out of volcanic rock. In fact it looks like a mansion on a California soap opera, with slanted roofs and a balcony overlooking the sea. Thuy knows every room by heart—the kitchen where all the heart-to-heart conversations between Sung and his lifelong nanny took place, the den where the girl of the week instigated her seductions.

When Jun took her there for the first time, she didn't recognize it. It was during a lashing windstorm, and Jun carried an umbrella that he tried to keep between them and the driving rain. The mansion was only depicted on television during sunny days or clear, moonlit nights, not when waves were crashing onto the balcony. She didn't ask, but she felt that Jun had chosen to show her the mansion in this different context, not as a fantasy house but as a real sanctuary. She left with a greater appreciation of the place, and of her husband's spirit.

He will not forbid her, but he will try to use her dreams. She has gone alone to the mansion a couple of times since Jun took her, when the weather was fair. Now, during another harsh windstorm, he takes her again. Although on this day it is closed to tourists, Jun knows the owner, who gives him a key. He takes Thuy to the balcony where she can feel the mist from the waves below. He points to the roiling sea. "Right now, there is probably a *haenyeo* out there drowning," he says. Underneath his raincoat Thuy can see his baby-blue sweater made out of a wispy type of cotton that flares at the sleeves, just like the one Sung wore. Jun has grown his hair out over the last year and the back of it is fluttering in the wind, while his bangs stick to his forehead, the rain darkening the steel grey. With his flapping scarf and smile, Thuy knows just what part of her imagination he is trying to appeal to.

...

Not every day with the mermaids is spent diving. Sometimes Thuy stays on land with Yuri to entertain the tourists. Thuy's relative youth and grasp of English are advantages here, and she finds she can get the tourists to relate to her. She and Yuri have developed a shtick whereby Yuri will pull a live octopus from a red bucket to Thuy's horror and waving hands. As Thuy tries to rescue it, Yuri will chew its rubbery head off, stretching it like taffy. Thuy spends whole mornings entertaining tourists with a dry wetsuit on.

But even on mornings when she is diving, Thuy still spends most of the day with Jun, stopping by the market before heading home to make him lunch. She knows this is not enough for him. And she knows that he will not stop her from diving, not outright, though he always has a silent plan.

Not so long ago Thuy's mother emailed her that Jun had stopped sending her the red envelopes. Thuy had not heard from her mother for the longest time, and then to get this in her inbox about her mother's desperate straits — about the forbidding cost of bare necessities, about the loans from neighbours left unpaid, about the DVDs that her mother can no longer buy even on discount. Whatever Thuy had once made in the market she gave to her mother. Now her mother is alone, fending for herself. Thuy wonders who will be climbing up to the tin roof of their hut to replace the sandbags that secure it now that Thuy is longer able to.

Jun can only smile. "I'm trying my best," he says, "but I told you, I have to hire extra help since you're not around. I can only give what I can. Maybe if you came back to me."

"But I haven't left."

Thuy has not even mentioned to Jun the one million won that she needs to raise to join the fishing cooperative that the mermaids belong to. Now that the others know she is serious about doing *muljil* — the *haenyeo*'s work — she must pay the money to continue diving with them. Perhaps, she thinks, with just a bit more practice, she'll be able to pay her dues in abalone. She will get better, and she will send her mother the little red envelopes herself, and she will still have enough left over to pay for the extra farmhand that Jun claims he needs.

These days she leaves the house even when there is no diving, when the storms are so severe that the tourists stay away and the boats stay moored. On such mornings she will go to Yuri's house, one of the old thatched huts for which the government helps pay for upkeep under its heritage laws. Thuy worries about her friend, who lives alone, and often finds her on the floor, too sore from diving to do anything but play solitaire. High above is a shelf lined with dusty books in Korean, English, and French. Thuy recognizes *A Tale of Two Cities*. *Du côté de chez Swann* is another. Yuri catches the upward drift of Thuy's eyelashes.

"I have always wanted to speak different languages," says Yuri.

"To be able to speak to the tourists?"

"Sometimes entertaining the tourists is just my excuse to practise languages, nothing more. Do you understand?"

Thuy nods, though she is not sure she does. Ever since Thuy landed on this island she has been speaking less, using language less. Not even her Korean has improved much. She's been skipping the classes.

"I thought of being a teacher when I was young, but I couldn't stand still in a room," says Yuri. Now she is lying flat on her back. Yuri refuses Thuy's help around the little hut, does not even let her put the teakettle on the stove, but finally relents when Thuy insists on at least massaging her aching joints, from her ankles to her brittle shoulders, and keeping her company on the blanket spread on the floor, playing cards.

"I will pay your dues to the *muljil*," says Yuri. "You can pay me back. Low interest." Thuy does not need to explain to Yuri why she is so grateful for this gesture of friendship. Yuri, it seems, has a sixth sense about what is going on behind the walls of Thuy's home.

"I've known him since he was a boy," says Yuri of Jun. "I worked on his farm, a long time ago, when his mother was still alive." That was how she had broken her hip, falling off an orange tree in Jun's orchard.

"Has he changed?"

"Always the same," says Yuri. "He was after my daughter, you know. She lives in Busan now, where she went to university. She's coming to visit me this weekend with her fiancé."

Thuy does not say anything at first.

"Don't worry, it was nothing," says Yuri. "Jun was after a lot of girls before he met you."

They play a couple of hands, and then Thuy says she has to get home to make her husband lunch. "Come have dinner with us," says Thuy. "This weekend."

"But my daughter."

"Bring her too. I will make Vietnamese food. Jun will make Korean food."

"I didn't know he cooked! His mother did everything for him."

"Then you are curious."

Yuri gingerly raises herself from the floor and brings

down a small jewellery box from her drawer. Inside are two unadorned pearls, large and faintly shimmering—a milky confection with a hint of silver.

"These earrings are a little too large for a young woman like you to wear, but hold on to them as part of your debt."

"I don't understand."

"A family heirloom," says Yuri. "My great-grandmother dived for these pearls herself, the kind you would never find today. Wear them when you are diving. They'll keep you, my investment, safe." Then Yuri's eyes brighten with a thought. "Oh, wear them to dinner. I want to see them on you."

When Thuy comes home in the rain, Jun is waiting, scared sick. He thinks that Thuy has been diving in this stormy weather. Thuy says nothing to disabuse him of this notion. Instead, she tells him that she would like to invite her own friends to dinner for once.

...

Thuy has bought a fresh cloth for the dinner, to cover the same table that Jun uses for his card games. Jun, meanwhile, digs out a clay urn that is buried in the yard containing kimchi. She and Jun share the same cutting board and stove to make their separate dishes. He makes pickled vegetables and raw seafood, and she makes imperial rolls and crepes made out of mung beans, a specialty from her village. There is a frantic rush just before the guests arrive and their ingredients contaminate each other's dishes; the harsh odour of his garlic has infiltrated her delicate crepes, while her fish sauce has masked the true flavours of his seafood. Both work grimly through to the knock on the door.

Yuri is at the front door, dressed in pearls and a blue dress. Between her armpit and arm is a Louis Vuitton handbag that her daughter has just brought to her. She looks like a stately grandmother. She smiles at Thuy, then looks up at Jun. "I used to be your farmhand, and now I am your guest," she says.

Yuri's daughter, meanwhile, looks as though she has just stepped out of a boardroom. Beside her is her fiancé, a tall man wearing a seersucker suit, a material that Thuy has never seen in her life. He is bearing a bottle of champagne in one hand and a Riesling in the other, bows tied on each. They are both around Thuy's age. This man, his name is Insuk, hands Thuy the bottles of wine and she just stares at them, as if scared of dropping them, until Yuri gestures to the refrigerator.

"These wines are to be chilled," says Yuri, then takes the bottles while Thuy returns to the kitchen.

Thuy feels as if she is a waitress in a tavern as she and Jun scamper to serve their guests. In their rush to wash the fish sauce and garlic off their hands, they butt heads at the sink. She worries about the draft in their house that she has just started getting used to. It is some time before Thuy is able to join the table. Thuy learns that Yuri's daughter is a certified public accountant and that Insuk is a management consultant. Thuy has no idea what a management consultant is, or what distinguishes a "certified public" accountant from any other. What they both do sounds so abstract and glamorous.

The whole point of the dinner is to see what Jun is like around this girl whom he once courted, but the two largely ignore each other. Instead, Insuk and Yuri's daughter want to hear from the Vietnamese wife, and they are impressed by Thuy's English. Yuri's daughter speaks English as well, the best English that a Korean university could provide, though she cannot get rid of her Jeju accent. Insuk's English, though, is perfect. He went to university in Canada.

"Everything tastes wonderful," says Yuri's daughter. "Though I'm surprised there's no abalone." She is smiling keenly at Thuy.

"You always hated abalone," says Yuri.

"That's not fair. If I did, I don't anymore. I've learned to appreciate it."

"That's because your tastes are more expensive now," says Yuri.

Thuy asks Insuk if he's read *Anne of Green Gables*, because that it is all she knows in relation to Canada. Yuri's daughter laughs. "That's a children's book for girls," she says. Insuk nods his head and gives Thuy a warm, manly smile, both reassuring and pitying. Whatever it is that a management consultant does, Thuy is sure he does it well.

"What is a 'kindred spirit'?" says Thuy, continuing a conversation that she has momentarily forgotten these people were never a part of.

"I have no idea," says Yuri's daughter.

"It's simple," says Insuk. From under the table he takes his fiancée's hand then raises it, places it over his heart. He gives Thuy a wink, which to Thuy is all of Western culture contained in one gesture.

"She's learning how to dive," says Yuri.

"It's such a shame," says Yuri's daughter in English. "The waste of another good mind." It takes a moment for Thuy to realize that they are speaking about her.

"Shush," says Yuri, then she says something in Korean to her daughter. All the while Jun smiles as if he has no idea what they are talking about. In a gentlemanly manner Insuk steers the women to other topics. Jun does not say much during the dinner, and perhaps to draw him out, Insuk asks him about the farm. They talk mostly in Korean, though sometimes Insuk throws out English terms like "diminishing returns," which are equally foreign to Thuy, and Jun nods his head as if he is about to purchase something from this man.

When her guests run out of things to say, Thuy fills the gap in the conversation in the only way she knows. She talks about television.

"*Winter Nocturne!*" says Yuri's daughter. "That used to be my favourite show."

"Whatever happened to that actor who played Sung?" says Insuk.

"You don't remember the scandal?"

"The scandal—of course!"

"You must have forgotten because it was so embarrassing," says Yuri's daughter.

"Something to do with prostitutes and laser tag."

"Please don't remind me. He was a Presbyterian too, remember."

"Allegedly."

Thuy wishes she had never heard any of this. Sung never had an existence outside the show. The whole evening becomes strange. It is strange eating Vietnamese food with Riesling, which they only have mugs for. Thuy covers her face with a napkin.

"What's wrong?" says Yuri's daughter.

Thuy drops her napkin and stares this girl down. "Your fiancé could play Sung," says Thuy. "He is even better than the original. He just needs to grow his hair."

Yuri's daughter gives Thuy a dirty look, and Yuri looks amused. Insuk smiles courageously at Thuy. Jun asks Thuy what is going on, but Thuy ignores him. Thuy can tell that Jun wants their guests to leave, to resume his life with her. He has the gift satchel of mandarins ready. But as the evening draws on, and the champagne is uncorked and drunk out of mugs, Insuk begins looking at Thuy with an open gaze that Thuy returns. This man is so young, Thuy thinks. His whole life is waiting. In another time, in another world, she thinks.

...

Yuri tells her how much harder it is to harvest abalone these days. You need to swim farther and farther away from the cove. Now a ship takes you to them. The real diving takes place away from the tourists.

Before dawn, Yuri picks Thuy up at the farmhouse. Jun is still asleep when Thuy jumps on the back of Yuri's motorbike. She feels like a rebellious teenager holding on to Yuri's waist. They head over to a warehouse where the hum of motorcycle engines echoes off the tin walls. The mermaids change into their suits inside the warehouse. There is the cheerful, incomprehensible chatter of women preparing for work. When Thuy asks Yuri what it is they are talking about, Yuri tells her it is always about the same thing. "Money and our aching joints," she says, laughing. A toothless *haenyeo* points at Thuy's face before pointing at her own. "She says enjoy your smooth skin now," says Yuri. "Soon it will be lined like ours."

They climb down rocks, a shortcut to the dock, and there are cries of pain among the women as they lift their feet tentatively around the jagged formations. Once Thuy helps Yuri to the dock, she clambers up to help another mermaid down. They all board a motorboat operated by a man who looks to be Jun's age. On the deck of the boat they all huddle together, knee to knee, rubbing their ankles back to life or wiping dirt off their diving masks with mugwort. One of the women stuffs the green tendrils of mugwort into both her nostrils, to keep the abrasive salt air out of her hacking lungs. Yuri starts a chant that builds down the line, before the boat stops and the mermaids jump into the sea feet first.

They shed their age with each thrust of their hips deeper into the water, so that by the time they reach the craggy bottom they are young women again, the movement of their joints as smooth as the sea itself. Thuy, who has been building up her stamina so that she can stay under the water for over a minute, has to swim up for a breath before diving down again. The mermaids have entrusted her with an abalone knife. A minute is both nothing and forever. After a minute Thuy feels as though she has lived a lifetime under the water and is down to her last breath, but it takes her that long just to orient herself upside down, never mind trying to spot the abalone with their black shells hidden in the crevices of the black rocks.

The key, the mermaids tell her, is to find the gleam of their lips from under their shells. By the time she finds her first one, her lungs are about to explode. The key is to wedge the knife under the abalone's foot, and to do so quickly before it can fasten itself more firmly onto the rock. Her hands, though, tremble desperately, and her blade simply taps the abalone's shell, awakening it. By the time she gets the blade underneath the creature, it is too late, it will not budge. Thuy is now seeing stars in her eyes from both anger and lack of breath, and she stabs at the abalone on the underside of its shell, trying to wrench it from the rock. She destroys the creature, rendering it useless, and as white strands of its innards float off, Thuy heads back to the surface.

When the mermaids float back up, it is to deposit yet another abalone into the net tied to their floating red basket. When they break the surface and let out a whistle, it is the sound of pure victory. This they do with a mechanical compulsion. Meanwhile, Thuy's net lies empty. Already, after half an hour of submerging and then re-emerging, she is exhausted, and cannot tell anymore which part of the world is right side up.

Finally, just when her face is about to freeze into a rictus from holding her breath for yet another interminable moment, she finds her technique. She is developing an eye for the abalone, the subtle glitter they give off. Her knife slides easily beneath one of them and she pulls it whole off the rock. She finds her second wind. When she breaks the surface with an abalone, she gives her own victorious yelp.

For the next half-hour she is so caught up in her new-found power, almost drunk on it, that she does not notice that the current has pulled her away from the other divers. Now she can only see a few feet in front of her — it is as if she has entered a dark cave. She looks above her and the sunlight is blocked by a thick blanket of kelp. There is no light to reach for as she thrusts her hips upwards, only more kelp, enough to wrap her whole body, to mummify her.

The last thing she remembers is the glint of a knife blade cutting through the thick kelp, untangling her from it. Yuri's arms are wrapped around her, helping her to the surface. When she is back aboard the boat, throwing up water, she is crying and apologizing to Yuri.

"Don't worry, you did well. You didn't die."

Thuy takes off her cowl and removes the pearl earrings, but Yuri will not take them back.

"They're yours. My daughter didn't notice them on you at all that night. Do you remember?"

"Maybe she was just pretending not to notice."

"Is that better?"

Back in the warehouse, as the mermaids take off their rubber suits, the talk among them is merrier—not about death or their aching joints, but how the ocean has opened herself so generously to them this day. When they smile at Thuy and put their hands warmly on her knee and give her advice on technique, Thuy also forgets how close to death she was. She believes, for this moment, that she has made it through purgatory.

...

She cannot escape the sight and smell of oranges. They are everywhere, and not just in her backyard, not just in every crevice of her house, where they roll out of crates and down the kitchen floor, but in the city, in every storefront window, it seems, in every gift box. They are the gift of the island—small and sweet, with a peel so bright that she wonders if the whole fruit is actually made out of wax. Around the house she has taken to plugging her nose with mugwort to keep out the smell of the citrus. Her only escape from this land is beneath the sea.

Acknowledgements

I owe my thanks to many dear people who have helped me along the journey to publishing this book.

Thanks to my editor, Bethany Gibson, for believing in these stories and for her tireless and deeply insightful work to help me improve them. Thanks also to John Sweet, my copy editor extraordinaire.

Thanks to my agent, Carolyn Swayze, for her invaluable tenacity.

Thanks to my writing teachers — Shannon Stewart, Kathryn Kuitenbrouwer, Lee Henderson, and the late Wayne Tefs. Your lessons have not been forgotten.

Thanks to the Asian Canadian Writers' Workshop for their continued support, and to the late Jim Wong-Chu for his sadly brief yet enduring mentorship.

Thanks to my parents, who arrived on these shores with little, and who worked tirelessly to provide for their children, and yet also to teach us to appreciate the wonderful and the glorious.

Thanks to my sisters, Adeline and Monique, and my brother, David — little, wise siblings who have let me share their fascinating lives. And thanks to Peter Klassen, my best man and close reader.

Thanks to my wife, Sowon, for her love and best friendship, which have endured despite her reading all my first drafts. And thanks to my daughters, Margo and Oona, for always getting their father up when he is down (especially on cartoon Saturdays).

Earlier versions of most of these stories have appeared in the following journals: the *New Quarterly*, *EVENT*, the *Malahat Review*, *Prairie Schooner*, *Ricepaper*, and *Prairie Fire*. I want to thank the editors of these journals for their keen eyes and encouragement: Pamela Mulloy, Kim Jernigan, Anna Ling Kaye, Ian Cockfield, Shashi Bhat, Kwame Dawes, Ashley Strosnider, Rhonda Batchelor, and Andris Taskans. I would also like to thank Anita Chong, who edited two of these tales for *The Journey Prize Stories*.

The folk stories that appear in "Toad Poem" and "Mayfly" are found in *Vietnamese Folk-Tales: Satire and Humour* by Huu Ngoc (Ha Noi: The Gioi Publishers, 2010). Thanks to my father, Cam-Loi Huynh, for researching Vietnamese-language versions of these folk tales and providing me with their translations. My father is also responsible for translating the verses from *The Tale of Kieu* that appear in "The Forbidden Purple City."

The following is a list of other books that I found particularly useful while researching for several of my stories:

Brigham, Robert K. *ARVN: Life and Death in the South Vietnamese Army*. Lawrence: University Press of Kansas, 2006.

Do, Thien. *Vietnamese Supernaturalism: Views from the Southern Region*. New York: RoutledgeCurzon, 2003.

Hickey, Gerald Cannon. *Village in Vietnam*. New Haven, CT, and London: Yale University Press, 1964.

Long, Patrick Du Phuoc, and Laura Ricard. *The Dream Shattered: Vietnamese Gangs in America*. Lebanon, NH: University Press of New England, 1997.

Nguyen, Du. *The Tale of Kieu*. Translated by Huynh Sanh Thong. New Haven, CT, and London: Yale University Press, 1983.

Pham, Quyen Phuong. *Hero and Deity: Tran Hung Dao and the Resurgence of Popular Religion in Vietnam*. Chiang Mai: Mekong Press, 2009.

Truong, Buu Lam. *A Story of Vietnam*. Parker, CO: Outskirts Press, 2010.

Turner, Karen Gottschang, and Phan Thanh Hao. *Even the Women Must Fight: Memories of War from North Vietnam*. New York: John Wiley & Sons, 1998.

Weist, Andrew. *Vietnam's Forgotten Army: Heroism and Betrayal in the ARVN*. New York and London: New York University Press, 2007.

Philip Huynh was born in Vancouver, BC, where his parents met after fleeing Vietnam during the war. A graduate of the University of British Columbia, Huynh is also a practicing lawyer.

Huynh's stories have been widely published in literary journals, including the *New Quarterly*, *EVENT*, *Prairie Schooner*, and the *Malahat Review*. His fiction has also been published in two editions of the Journey Prize anthology and cited for distinction in *The Best American Short Stories*. He is the winner of the Open Season Award from the *Malahat Review*, a Glenna Luschei *Prairie Schooner* Award, and the Jim Wong-Chu Emerging Writers Award from the Asian Canadian Writers' Workshop. He lives in Richmond, BC, with his wife and twin daughters.